TOYMAN

Space-wanderer Earl Dumarest is on the planet Toy, hoping he'll get information on the whereabouts of Earth, his lost home world. But nothing is given freely there and he must fight in the Toy Games to gain the information he needs. He's forced to be like a tin soldier in a vast nursery with a spoiled child in command — but there's nothing playful about the Games on Toy. Everything is only too real: pain, wounds, blood — and death . . .

E. C. TUBB

TOYMAN

Complete and Unabridged

LINFORD
Leicester

First published in Great Britain

First Linford Edition
published 2010

British Library CIP Data

Tubb, E. C.
    Toyman. - - (Linford mystery library)
    1. Science fiction.
    2. Large type books.
    I. Title II. Series
    823.9'14–dc22

    ISBN 978–1–44480–421–8

Published by
F. A. Thorpe (Publishing)
Anstey, Leicestershire

Set by Words & Graphics Ltd.
Anstey, Leicestershire
Printed and bound in Great Britain by
T. J. International Ltd., Padstow, Cornwall

This book is printed on acid-free paper

1

For thirty hours the sun had arched across the sky, baking the desert with its oven-heat, but now that it was night the temperature had already fallen to the point where water turns to ice. It would, Dumarest knew, fall even lower during the twenty-hour period of darkness. Toy was a world of violent extremes.

He crouched closer to the fire, watching as Legrain fed it with thorned scrub and shards of bleached and weathered bone. Around them a circle of rock both shielded the fire from casual view and reflected the heat. Above the piled stones the wind gusted with freezing chill, heavy with the odour of weed and brine, the sullen roar of crashing waves.

'A bad night,' said Legrain. 'But all nights are bad for the defeated.'

He carefully fed a fragment of bone to the flames. Like Dumarest, he wore a sleeved tunic of vivid scarlet reaching to his knees. A metal helmet and breastplate shone with the colour of gold. A belt at his waist supported a bag and scabbarded sword. Earlier in the day he had also carried a shield and spear, but both had been discarded in the conflict. Helmet, breastplate and tunic showed dents and slashes. Blood from a minor wound had dried on one cheek. Lit by the fire, his big-nosed face gave him the appearance of a dishevelled eagle.

'Warmth and rest,' he said. 'At night, in the arena, the lack of either can kill as surely as sword and spear.' He delved into his bag and produced a scrap of meat. He speared it on the tip of his sword and held it to the flames. 'A bargain,' he suggested. 'A share of my meat for a share of your water. You have water?'

Dumarest shook his canteen. It made a liquid sound.

'Good. It is agreed?'

'Yes,' said Dumarest. 'But how about Sachen?'

'The boy?' Legrain shrugged. 'Earl, my friend, you must accept what is to be. The lad is as good as dead. We did him no

2

favour carrying him as we did. It would be better to ease his passage. A pressure on the carotids — it would be a kindness.'

Dumarest made no comment, looking instead to where a third man lay against the shelter of the rock. He too wore a slashed tunic and golden helmet but had no breastplate. His breathing was stentorian and, though he shivered, his ebony skin shone with a dew of sweat.

'Water,' he gasped. 'Water.'

Dumarest rose, crossed toward him, touched his forehead. The skin burned like fire. He gently lifted the tunic and examined the blood-soaked rag tied and belted about the hips. The material of the tunic was thin plastic, useless to keep out the cold.

'Water,' croaked the wounded man. 'Please give me some water.'

'No,' said Legrain.

'Shut up,' said Dumarest. He uncorked his canteen and, supporting Sachen's head, poured a thin trickle between the parched lips. 'Steady,' he urged as the man tried to snatch the canteen. 'Too much will be bad for you.' He set aside the canteen. 'How do you feel now, Jack?'

'Terrible.' The boy's eyes held a momentary clarity. 'Am I dying, Earl?'

'You're in a bad way,' said Dumarest. 'But you're not dead yet. Hang on, lad. You can get over this if you try.' He found the boy's hand, squeezed it, held it until his eyes clouded in fevered delirium.

'Mother,' muttered the boy. 'Mother, I'm cold, help me.'

'A spear in the guts,' said Legrain as Dumarest returned to his place by the fire. 'Without antibiotics or medical aid the end is a foregone conclusion. Pain, fever, delirium and death.' He turned his scrap of meat, sniffing at the odour. 'He should have made better use of his shield,' he commented. 'His shield and his legs. To stand and fight the way he did was foolish. He didn't stand a chance.'

'He did his best,' said Dumarest.

Legrain shrugged. 'It obviously wasn't good enough. You now, you fought well, I watched you often.'

'I fought to stay alive,' said Dumarest coldly. 'But we both had an advantage over the boy. He wears nothing but fabric

4

beneath his tunic.'

'While you and I wear metal-mesh buried in the plastic of our clothing.' Legrain nodded. 'Yes, Earl, I noticed that. I noticed too that you did your best to protect Sachen. Are you so close?'

Dumarest was curt. 'We travelled together.'

'On Low passage?' Legrain turned his meat. 'It would be Low,' he mused. 'You, an experienced traveller, and he, a novice perhaps on his first journey. A bad end to a short life, Earl,' he said seriously. 'But it happens, my friend. It happens.'

Yes, thought Dumarest bleakly. It happens all too often. Youngsters with adventure in their hearts and the galaxy to roam. A million worlds and adventure waiting at the end of each journey. Cheap travel if you were willing to accept riding doped, frozen and ninety per cent dead. Waiting also to accept the fifteen per cent death rate. One journey, he thought, and Sachen had used up his life. Not in the ship but on this insane world where men were set to fight each other for the entertainment of those who ruled. Fight and die and rot in the sand and scrub of the arena.

He rose and stared into the darkness, narrowing his eyes against the impact of the wind. How many other fires burned on the desert? he wondered. The victors had gone, airlifted away, now feasting and enjoying the fruits of success. The losers? Those who had survived had the battle still to finish: the struggle against the dark and cold, their wounds, fatigue, the voracious nocturnal life lurking in the sand. Unless they won that battle only their accoutrements and bones would greet the new day.

* * *

The meat was hard, seared, tasteless, but it was hot and provided sustenance. Dumarest chewed, passed Legrain his canteen, felt himself begin to relax from the fatigue of the day. But relaxing brought its own problems. His uniform and clothing had protected him against penetration but not against bruising. He ached from head to foot.

'Why?' he demanded. 'Why this non-sense?'

'The battle?' Legrain swallowed and took a drink of water. 'You should know, my friend. You wore the red and gold against the green and silver.'

'But not from choice,' said Dumarest bitterly. He glanced to where Sachen lay whimpering against the rock. 'We landed yesterday at dusk. Guards were waiting as we left the field. The choice was simple; show the cost of a double High passage or stand trial, be convicted and sentenced to a year of forced labour as a vagrant. That or agree to enlist for one engagement. A day,' he said, 'against a year. What choice is that?'

'For the boy the difference between life and death,' pointed out Legrain. 'But I see your point. One engagement and then money and the freedom of Toy. An attractive offer, especially to someone travelling Low.' He bit at the last of his meat. 'You were unfortunate, my friend. You arrived at a bad time.'

A bad time on a bad planet, thought Dumarest. There were too many such

7

places. Dead ends, restricted worlds, planets where transients were unwelcome and unwanted. Societies in which there was no place for a man who simply wanted to work, to build up the cost of a passage, to move on to somewhere new.

Legrain probed thoughtfully at his teeth. 'I too was given that same choice and, like you, I elected to fight.' He smiled as he met Dumarest's eyes. 'That's right, my friend. I too am a traveller. Or was,' he corrected. 'I visited a score of worlds before bad luck brought me to Toy. Toy,' he mused. 'An odd name, is it not? Legend has it that Director Conrad of Grail, on learning of the birth of his first-born son, promised to give the lad a world as a plaything. This is it.'

Dumarest made no comment.

'The stockholders are jaded,' said Legrain. 'They seek always for new pleasures, new sensations. Insults must be avenged in blood and men must be found to spill that blood. A hundred, five hundred, sometimes a thousand men facing each other with primitive weapons. A fine spectacle of blood and death and pain. Did you not see the rafts floating safely above?'

'I was busy,' said Dumarest dryly. 'But I saw them.'

'Spectators,' said Legrain. 'Gamblers. Vultures at the feast. Lovers seeking new titivations.' He stabbed at the fire with the tip of his sword. 'Rest,' he said abruptly. 'I will stand the first watch.'

Dumarest stretched, lying beside the fire, feeling the heat warm his face. The breastplate was uncomfortable but he didn't think of removing it. In this place protection was of prime importance. He closed his eyes, seeing again the taut faces, the wild eyes, flashing steel, dust, gaping wounds, the sudden gush of blood. In memory he heard again the rasp of breath, the shouts, screams, clash of weapons, tasted the swirling dust, felt his overstrained muscles jerk to sympathetic exertion.

Irritably he turned, opening his eyes and looking up at the stars. The sight was disturbing. There was something wrong about the sky: the stars were too thin, too scattered. He missed the sheets and curtains of brilliance, the nebulae, the close-packed suns of the centre. And yet, if he could trust memory, the planet he sought had skies much as this. Dark skies with a single moon, few stars and a band of light tracing its way from horizon to horizon. Stars assembled in vaguely remembered patterns, cold, remote, burning in the stillness of the night. So far, so distant it seemed incredible they could ever be reached.

He jerked, aware that he had fallen asleep, nerves taut with the consciousness of danger. He looked around. Legrain had vanished and the fire had shrunk to a glowing ember. Shivering, he rose, drew his sword, held the yard strip of edged and pointed steel ready in his hand. He did not like the weapon: the blade was too long, too clumsy, impossible to throw with any force or accuracy. Transferring it to his left hand he drew the ten-inch knife from his boot, poising it as his eyes searched the darkness.

Against his rock Sachen muttered in his delirium. 'Mother,' he said. 'Mother.'

'Easy,' said Dumarest softly. He stepped

across the fire, staring into the starlit dimness. Light and shadow made a vague chiaroscuro of blurred and indeterminate detail. Abruptly a stone rattled off to one side. Legrain? Dumarest faced the direction of the sound, ears strained, eyes narrowed to catch the slightest hint of movement. A second rattle came, this time closer and then something, a shadow, the disturbance of the air, primitive instinct, caused him to duck and spring to one side.

A spear flashed through the space in which he had been standing.

A second followed it, thrust by an indistinct shape rushing from the darkness, the broad blade aimed directly at his eyes. Dumarest swung up his left hand, parrying the shaft with the sword, his right hand thrusting forward with the ten-inch blade of his knife. He felt the jolt, the stench of foul breath on his cheeks, the weight of a lunging body. Caught off-balance he fell, rolled across the fire, sprang to his feet in a shower of sparks.

'You fool!' he said, 'Don't . . . '

The spear lunged at him again, held

11

rigid by two hands backed by wild eyes, a gaping mouth. Dumarest had lost both sword and knife. He dropped to one knee, rose as the blade passed his shoulder, gripped the shaft with both hands as he twisted aside. Momentum carried his assailant forward, toppled him over as he clung grimly to the spear. Dumarest pulled it loose, lifted it, thrust down with the blade. Tearing it free, he spun to face the sound of crunching sand.

'Easy, my friend.' Legrain came from the darkness beyond the circle of stone. He carried a heap of thorned scrub in his hands. He threw down the fuel, then raked together the embers, blew them to life, fed the dancing flames. In the light he looked down at what Dumarest had killed. 'A man,' he said. 'He doesn't look it but that's what he is.' He stirred the body with his foot. 'A man who tried to survive.'

He was thin, emaciated, face masked by a heavy growth of beard. His clothing was an assortment of bulky rags overlaid with a dozen tunics of various colours. His helmet and breastplate were black.

Beneath the beard his face was mottled with sores. Eyes, open in death, shone reddish in the light of fire.

'A loser,' explained Legrain. 'Someone who managed to avoid the hunters. Hiding among the rocks, living on what he could find, driven insane by hardship and the poison in the local insects. He must have seen our fire.' He kicked again at the body. 'I saw the end of the fight,' he said. 'You were fast, Earl. I don't think I've ever seen anyone as fast.'

Dumarest bent down, searching the dead man. His knife had glanced from the breastplate and was buried to the hilt in the mass of clothing. He drew it out, wiped it, thrust it back in his boot. He sheathed his sword, stooped, gripped the dead man by the shoulders. 'Help me,' he said to Legrain.

Together they carried the body from the circle of stone, dumping it between two boulders.

'Tomorrow it will be gone,' said Legrain as they returned to the fire. 'The metal and bones will be all that remain.' Reaching the fire he sat down and warmed his hands. 'Tell me, Earl. Why did you come to Toy?'

Dumarest added more scrub to the fire. 'On business.'

'Here that can only have one meaning,' mused Legrain. 'The wealth of the planet rests on the computer.' He looked curiously at Dumarest. 'What reason could a traveller have for consulting the library?'

'The same as any man's,' said Dumarest. 'To ask a question and receive an answer.'

'The question?'

Dumarest hesitated, then mentally shrugged. What difference could it make to confide in the man? It could even be to his advantage. Legrain was a traveller and could have learned what he wanted to know. 'I am looking for a planet,' he said. 'The planet Earth. Do you know of it?'

'Earth?' Legrain frowned. 'An odd name for a world. Who would call a planet by a name like that? As well call it soil or dirt or loam. Earth.' He chuckled. 'Earl, my friend, you surely jest.'

'You have never heard of the name?'

'The name, yes.' Legrain leaned forward, scooped up a handful of sand, let it trickle between his fingers. 'This is sand. Is there a planet with such a name? On the mainland I would have picked up a handful of earth. You see the analogy?'

It was another defeat, one of a countless number, but Dumarest wasn't disappointed. What men had forgotten the Library must remember. If the knowledge was available at all it could well be here on Toy in the banks of the famous computer.

He turned as Sachen whimpered and suddenly called out. The boy was no longer sweating. His dark skin held a flat, greyish palor beneath the pigment. 'Water!' he croaked. 'Water!'

Legrain dropped his hand to the canteen. 'No,' he said. 'It would be a waste.'

Dumarest looked at the hand, then at the big-nosed face.

'All right,' said Legrain. 'Why not? Tomorrow we shall all be dead.'

Dumarest rose, fed the boy the last of the water, threw aside the canteen as he sat facing Legrain across the fire. The

15

shifting light stained his face with dancing colour, accentuating the hard lines and planes, the strong jaw and mouth. It was the face of a man who had learned early to rely on no one but himself. Legrain moved uneasily beneath the impact of his eyes.

'Explain,' said Dumarest. 'What do you mean when you say that we shall be dead?'

Legrain shrugged. 'I mean nothing but the truth, my friend. Three times have I fought in the arena. Twice I was fortunate to be on the winning side. Each time I lived high, for there were few survivors and so the share of each was all the greater. But this time I chose the wrong side. This time I die.'

'You are not dead yet,' reminded Dumarest.

'Listen.' Legrain drew a pattern in the sand, a rough circle joined to a curve by a thin line. 'This,' he said, tapping the circle, 'is the arena. This line is the neck of land joining it to the mainland. Across it is the Barrier, wired, fenced, guarded with towers, impossible to pass without

16

permission. Around the arena are cliffs three hundred feet high falling to the rocks and the sea. If you descend them there is only rock and water waiting to tear out your life. No boats. No way of escape. We lost,' he emphasised. 'The red and gold were beaten, scattered, smashed to ruin. And we fought for the red and gold.'

'So?'

'How do you make men fight?' demanded Legrain. 'Pay them well? True, but that is only the carrot. High pay and rich rewards if you win. But how to make men really fight? A carrot isn't enough; there must also be a whip. The whip is death. You win or you die, That is why it isn't enough to fight to stay alive. You must fight to win. For, if you do not win, you die. And,' he added grimly, 'we did not win.'

'We can escape,' said Dumarest.

'How? Do you intend to grow wings and fly across the sea? Become invisible so as to pass the Barrier? Hide here among the rocks without food or water? Have you wondered why you've seen no old-dead, only bones? Look at the bones, my friend. See the marks on them. At night the arena vomits forth its own life. Only a fire keeps them away; the light and warmth delude them into believing that it's day. But for how long could you live with a fire alone?'

Dumarest looked into darkness where they had dumped the body.

'Do you want to end like that?' Legrain had guessed his thoughts. 'Perhaps you could survive for a while, but the end is inevitable. No,' he ended. 'Tomorrow we die.'

'Are you so in love with death?'

'No, my friend, but I am a realist. I accept what has to be.' Legrain stretched himself before the fire. 'Your watch, Earl. Wake me when you become tired.'

Dumarest nodded, not answering, sitting tensed and thoughtful as he stared at the slowly wheeling stars.

★   ★   ★

Dawn came with a flush of rose, of pink and gold and crimson, of spears of violet and tinted clouds of cerise drifting against an azure sky. The sun lifted from beneath the sea, bringing warmth to thaw the rime and frost from the region. And with the dawn came the antigrav rafts, the hunters, the men and women eager for the kill.

They came from the north, beyond the Barrier, riding a comfortable fifty feet above the ground, too high for danger from below and, like dogs chasing rats, they sought those who had survived the frozen night.

'Target practice,' said Dumarest. He stood watching, hearing the sharp, spiteful sounds as the hunters stood in their rafts firing primitive missile weapons at the survivors below. 'But why?' he demanded. 'Why kill when those men could be put to better use?'

'Orders of the Toymaster,' said Legrain. In the dawn his face was pale, peaked, the dried blood ugly on his cheek. 'No reprieve — a man wins in the arena or he dies. One way or another he dies.' He looked to where Sachen lay slumped against the stone. Sometime in the night the boy had died. 'He is a lucky one.'

Dumarest grunted, annoyed at the pessimism. He drew his sword and examined it. The hilt was a simple crosspiece. Two of them could be lashed together to make a six-foot bow. Using a spear as an arrow perhaps . . . ? He tested the blade, swore as the metal curved and remained bent. Cheaply produced like the armour, which was little better than plated tin. Tin soldiers, he thought bleakly. Toys in a giant nursery with a spoiled child in command. But the pain had been real enough, the wounds, the blood and death. There had been nothing childish about those.

'What are you doing?' Legrain watched, his eyes huge with their smudging of shadowed fatigue. 'A bow? What will you use for an arrow?'

'Nothing.' Dumarest threw down the sword. 'The metal isn't good enough,' he explained. 'But we need something to reach those rafts.' He stood thinking, then snapped his fingers. 'Got it! Find me some stones. Smooth and round and about the size of an egg. Hurry!'

As Legrain searched, Dumarest took

off the useless helmet and breastplate, stripped off the tunic and slashed it with his knife. He plaited, knotted and hefted the crude sling. Legrain returned with the stones. Dumarest fitted one into his crude weapon, spun it around over his head, let the stone fly. It arched into the sky well above the desired height.

'That thing,' said Legrain. 'Can you aim it?'

'I used to be able to use a sling,' said Dumarest, remembering. 'When I was a boy back on my home world.'

Back on Earth, he thought, where small game was scarce and noise to be avoided. But that had been a long time ago now. How long? There was no way of telling. During the long journeys sleeping in Low or doped with quick time in High, time was a swift-passing phenomenon. Biologically his time was measured in decades, chronologically in centuries. He could only hope that he had not lost all his skill.

'They're coming,' said Legrain, squinting at the rafts. 'Heading this way. If they get suspicious, rise higher . . . '

'What are their weapons?' Dumarest

crouched against the rock, the grey of his clothing blending with the stone. 'Missiles, I know, but high-velocity or what?'

'Powerful,' said Legrain. 'I won the last two times, remember? A few of us were invited to join a clean-up squad, collecting trophies, things like that.' He didn't look at Dumarest. 'Mostly they aim for the body, and those bullets went right through.'

'All right,' said Dumarest. 'Get rid of that uniform. Wearing it makes you too good a target.' He stared at the oncoming rafts. One had swerved and was heading directly toward them. Somehow he had to divert the attention of the occupants, gain time to use the sling. He looked at Sachen. The boy was dead, nothing could hurt him now. Urgently he called to Legrain, told him what he wanted. The man hesitated, then nodded.

'All right,' he said. 'But, Earl, don't miss.'

'I'll do my best,' promised Dumarest.

He loaded the sling, put other stones to hand, stood crouched against the stone as Legrain heaved the dead boy from within the circle. The sun caught his vivid red tunic against the brown and grey. From the air he looked like a man, wounded, helpless, signalling for aid. The raft veered, presenting its side to the target as Dumarest began to rotate his sling.

The raft drifted closer. A voice echoed from it. 'Hands off, people, this one is mine!'

A man appeared at the side, the upper part of his body above the low railing. He lifted a rifle to his shoulder, aiming as Legrain half-fell behind the body of Sachen. Dumarest stepped free of the stone, air whining as he spun the sling, releasing the stone as the man fired.

The bullet hit the dead boy, knocking him sidewise from Legrain's grasp, leaving Legrain a clear target. The stone, winging upward, smashed the marksman just below the breastbone. He doubled, rifle falling out and down as he fell backward into the raft. Legrain ran for it, caught it as it fell, turned and raced back to where Dumarest whirled his reloaded sling. Fire spurted from the raft as he released the second stone. Legrain stumbled, fell,

23

the rifle flying from his hands. Dumarest dropped the sling, caught the rifle, dived for shelter as bullets chipped splinters from the raft. The pilot, white-faced, froze his hands on the controls as Dumarest yelled up from the ground.

'Drop the raft! Drop it or I'll kill you!'

He tensed as the raft slowly lowered itself to the ground. Legrain, limping, came towards him.

'You've got them, Earl. You've got them!'

'Are you hurt?'

'No. They shot the heel off my boot.' Legrain edged forward as the raft came within reach. 'Now, Earl?'

'Now!'

They ran forward, jumped into the open body of the vehicle, searched it with quick glances. A dead man stared at them, a hole between his eyes. Another fought for breath as he lay in a pool of his own vomit, blood frothing from his mouth as broken ribs tore at his lungs. A third had an unrecognisable pulp for a face — the second stone had found a target. The pilot sat at his controls rigid with terror.

'Is that all?' snapped Dumarest.

'That's right, sir.' The pilot was shaking. 'That's all.'

'All right,' said Dumarest. 'Out.'

'But . . .'

'Out!' The pilot took one look at the bleak face and sprang from the raft to the desert. Dumarest turned, glared at Legrain. 'Don't waste time, man. Get them over the side.'

'A moment.' Legrain was busy rifling the bodies of the dead, the pockets of the injured. 'We'll need money,' he reminded. 'The means to buy a passage.' Grunting, he heaved them over the rail. 'All right, Earl. Take us up.' He relaxed as the raft climbed into the sky. 'We've done it,' he gloated. 'We've beaten the Toymaster.'

Dumarest was curt. 'Not yet, we haven't. Grab one of those rifles. Shoot anyone who comes too close.' He looked at the other man. 'You've been here longer than I have. What now?'

'Rise high, head out to sea, aim for the sun. We'll swing in a wide circle and hit the mainland well past the Barrier. The cliffs are rotten with caves. We'll find one

25

and hide out until dark or maybe until tomorrow. Then we'll head back into the city and arrange a passage. Mother Jocelyn will help us.'

Legrain laughed, a man reprieved from death.

2

Leon Hurl, Stockholder of Toy, woke two hours after dawn and lay staring at the patterned ceiling as he waited for the slave to bring his morning tea. It was going to be a busy day he decided. Aside from his normal duties there was the meeting of the Spinners Association, during which they would decide future production, among other things. This time, he hoped, they would avoid sterile rehashing of the obvious. They had already taken greater risks than he cared to think about. It would be easy to go just that little bit too far.

A discreet knock signalled the arrival of his tea. The girl was young, nubile and not adverse to his favours, but today she was disappointed. Leon had other things on his mind.

The phone hummed as he sipped the hot, spiced liquid. Irritably he reached out and hit the button. Mere Evan, a

27

fellow stockholder, stared at him from the screen. 'A bright day, Leon. Did I wake you?'

'No.'

'Then the offence is not as great as I feared. You accept my apology?' He didn't wait for Leon's nod; excitement shattering the formal routine of polite behaviour. 'Leon, we did it! We beat the Toymaster!'

Leon sighed. 'I know. And now I expect you want to call a special meeting of the cabal.'

'Well, yes,' admitted Evan. 'I thought that . . . '

'You think too much,' said Leon gently, 'and don't understand enough. The last thing we can afford is to call attention to ourselves. If Groshen ever guesses that we were aligned against him he would take violent action. Very violent.' He looked steadily at his caller. 'I made the wager. I shall collect the winnings. We shall discuss details at the regular meeting of the Association scheduled for later today. Or had you forgotten?'

Evan flushed.

'You are too eager,' said Leon. 'There is

no need of haste. The plan . . . '

'You are wrong, Leon,' interrupted Evan. 'Things aren't as they were. Did you know the Toymaster has a cyber in attendance?'

Leon frowned. 'Are you sure?'

'I saw him myself. His name is Creel. Why would Groshen want a cyber, Leon?'

Wrong question, thought Leon. What interest the Cyclan could have in Toy would be more to the point. The services they offer were here totally unnecessary. He smiled blandly at the anxious face on the screen. 'You worry too much Mere. We must do nothing without careful thought. This morning I will be at the factory. Later we shall meet as arranged. Until then do nothing.'

He killed the instrument and sat frowning on the edge of the bed. He was a broad stocky man with close-crimped hair and ebony features both showing his unsullied descent from the original settlers. Evan was too anxious, he thought. The man was getting to be a positive danger. And yet his news was important. A cyber? Here on Toy? The thing made little sense, but the man had to be taken into account. He must find out more about the sudden interest the Cyclan was taking in the planet.

Rising, he bathed, used a depilatory cream on his stubble, adjusted his hair. He seemed even broader dressed than he really was, wide epaulets extending his clavicles, a broad belt cinching his waist. Flared pants and boots of polished jet increased the illusion. Casually he slipped the ceremonial whip over his left wrist and his attire was complete.

Breakfast was a compote of juice, cereal and dried fruits washed down with more of his favourite spiced tea. His personal antigrav raft carried him from his home to the factory situated well beyond the limits of the town.

It was a huge place, the roof of the main hall soaring almost a hundred feet above the ground, the looms wide-spaced on the park-like floor. Despite the gusts of air blowing through the ventilators the place had an insect-smell, an acrid, musty odour. The air was still warm to compensate for the chill of the night; later it would become cool to check the heat of the day.

Leon paused in the shadow of a loom, watching, sensing rather than seeing the smooth efficiency of the place. The floor was clean, he noted, the weavers busy on their looms, overseers standing by with electronic goads. In the glare of the overhead lights the place was a shimmering blaze of colour.

Webmaster Vogel was busy entertaining a group of off-world buyers, giving them, Leon noted, the special treatment that was composed of deference, humour, explanation and a subtle implication that they knew as much as he did and could, if they wanted, do as well. That was ridiculous, of course. It took twenty years to make a webmaster and even then most of them couldn't be trusted to produce a new pattern.

'As you see, Gentles,' Vogel was saying, 'the weavers are mutated spiders genetically selected for size, dexterity and colour of thread. You will note the development of their spinnerets. We use the injection method of teaching. A selected weaver is trained to perform a certain task and, when it has mastered what is required, when it is required, a serum is drawn from its major ganglia and that serum injected into others of its kind. The 'memory' of the training is thus transmitted from one weaver to many others. The rest is a simple matter of setting up the looms, overseeing, feeding and all the rest of it.'

Simple, thought Leon wryly. The mere fact that the spiders could be trained at all was an achievement in itself. To get them to weave as they did was little short of miraculous.

'We have three hundred and seven regular pictorial designs,' continued the webmaster. 'And seven hundred and twenty-eight repetitious patterns of various sizes. Therefore carpets, wall coverings and dress fabrics can be made to suit any require-ment.' Vogel stooped, picked up a gossamer piece of fabric, a carpet large enough to cover a room. Crushing it into a ball, he held it with one clenched fist. Releasing it, it sprang open, unmarked and uncreased.

'The colours are inherent in the

material and so are permanent. Weight for weight the fabric is stronger than any plastic or metal alloy and, treated as it is, is both fire-and weatherproof. If you own nothing else, Gentles, you should possess a web of Toy. With it you have a tent, a cloak, a pattern to beguile the weary hours. A means of signalling if you are in distress, a soft embrace for a partner and something to leave your heirs.'

He had ventured close, thought Leon. Perhaps too close, for off-worlders were inclined to be touchy. Then they chuckled and he relaxed. Trust the webmaster to successfully gauge the tolerance of his audience. A man who could breed the irritable and ferocious arachnids would find human emotions child's play.

He caught the webmaster's eye, gestured with his head. Vogel made his apologies and came to where he was standing. 'Stockholder Hurl.'

'How is it going, Webmaster?'

'Well,' said Vogel. 'I think these buyers will look no further after they see what we have to offer.' He hesitated. 'May I be so bold as to offer my congratulations,

Stockholder? The battle,' he explained. 'I watched it yesterday on the screen. An obvious victory for the green and silver.'

Leon nodded his acknowledgment of the praise.

'I won myself the entire dividend of a total share,' said Vogel with pride. 'Are you wagering again, Stockholder?'

'No,' said Leon. 'And if you are wise neither will you. It would be a great pity to see you standing on the block to be sold for non-payment of debt.'

Familiarity and a conscious knowledge of his own value edged Vogel's tongue with impertinence. 'But you would buy me, Stockholder Hurl. Who else would train your weavers?'

'There are others,' said Leon sharply. Vogel was as dark-skinned as himself, but the smoothness of his hair told of his polluted descent. And, an even greater difference, the man held no stock. It would do no harm to remind him of the fact. 'Get put on the block,' he said deliberately, 'and I will buy you. That is true. But only to keep your skill from others. You would be put to work in the feeding pens. Good as you are, Web-master, that is how I would treat you. Remember it.'

'Yes, Stockholder.'

'You have offended me.' Leon brought the lash of his whip hard against the side of his leg. 'See that the offence is not repeated. Now return to your duties.'

Vogel bowed, shielding his eyes.

* * *

Outside the huge building Leon paused, breathing the crisp morning air, glad to be away from the looms. The mutated spiders provided a constant stream of wealth but even so he could not overcome a lifelong repugnance for the creatures. It stemmed, he thought, from the time his father had forced him to watch them feed. To gain energy they needed a diet high in protein and so had been bred with a taste for meat. Even now he could remember the screaming of the slaves. Broken men, criminals, the debris of the auctions it was true but men just the same.

He shook himself, such thoughts were dangerously weak. Things were what they were because the system was what it was. Before anything could be changed the system had to be shattered. Well, he corrected, not exactly that but altered to a major extent. It was long past the time when Groshen could really be permitted to wield the power that was his heritage. And yet the system was such that his power was virtually unbreakable.

In his office, Hurl touched a button. The screen lit with the pale face of a common worker. 'This is Stockholder Hurl,' said Leon shortly. 'The state of my account.'

'One moment, Stockholder.' A half-minute slid past. 'You still have five per cent of your last dividend to your credit, Stockholder.'

Five per cent, thought Leon, killing the phone. As much as that? He sat thinking. What more did he need? A new antigrav raft? More webbing for his palace? A few extra slaves? Deciding, he hit a button. The face of his social secretary looked from the screen.

'Elgar,' said Leon. 'Those embroideries of Sha'-Tung art. Buy them.'

'All of them, Stockholder?'

'As many as my credit will stand. Best to hurry,' he reminded. 'The next dividend is due in five days. But before the price rises.'

'As you order, Stockholder.'

Leon sighed as he turned from the screen. A frugal man, he hated this regular necessity of spending the last of his credit. And yet what else could he do? Unless spent it would be cancelled. On Toy a stockholder could not accumulate wealth.

The intercom hummed at his side. 'A man to see you, Stockholder,' said his receptionist. 'Are you available?'

'Has he an appointment?'

'No, Stockholder. But he is a monk of the Universal Brotherhood.'

'His name?'

'Brother Elas, Stockholder.'

Leon was intrigued. 'Send him in.'

Monks of the Universal Brotherhood were scarce on Toy. Some had set up a church close to the spacefield, others dispensed medicines and benedictions among the poor. Some even haunted the auction place, rattling their chipped bowls of cheap plastic in an endless plea for alms. What could they want with him?

'Charity, brother,' said the monk quietly when he shot the question. 'The gift of kindness from one member of humanity to another. The gift of life itself in all too many cases.'

Leon gestured to a chair. 'Such as?'

'There was a battle yesterday. Five hundred men fought in the arena. One hundred and ten survived to enjoy the victors' feast. What of the rest, brother?'

'They died.'

'Of cold, exposure and wounds,' agreed the monk. 'Many could have been saved had they medicine and fire, food and medical attention. Far more would have lived to see the dawn had we been permitted to render our services.'

'No.' Leon was emphatic. 'In the arena they either win or die.' He held up a hand to still the other's protest. 'It is not my ruling, Brother. Grego Groshen rules Toy. You must address your pleas to him, not to me. I am not the Toymaster.'

'You are a stockholder.'

'I and twenty million others.'

'But you hold more stock than most,' reminded the monk shrewdly, 'and so have greater influence. Please, brother, I beg your charity on behalf of those who cannot help themselves.'

Leon sat back in his chair, studying the monk in his rough, homespun robe. The man was cultured — his voice betrayed his education — and if rumour was correct he would be a master of the psychological arts. What made such a man content to wear a simple robe, crude sandals on naked feet? His eyes lifted to the close-cropped head, the thin ascetic face wreathed by the thrown-back cowl, the eyes deep-sunk in shadowed sockets.

'Listen,' he said abruptly. 'As yet you have given me no reason to help you. Answer one question to my satisfaction and I will, see what can be done. You accept the challenge?'

Brother Elas bowed his head. 'I accept.'

'Very well,' said Leon. He drew a deep breath. 'Give me one good reason why I should help you.'

The eyes of the monk met his own. 'Look at your fellow men, Stockholder. The slaves, the ruined men, the broken women, those stricken with disease and poverty. Look at them and remind yourself of one simple fact. Say it to yourself: There, but for the grace of God, go I.'

'Your creed?'

'Yes, brother. The day that all men look at others with that thought in mind the millennium will have arrived.'

Leon was ironic. 'Perhaps, but I do not think that many alive today will see it.'

'No, brother, that is true,' admitted the monk. 'But we do what we can.'

And what you do, thought Leon, is very well done. Somehow the man had made him feel guilty, a little ill at ease, and yet there was no reason for anger or impatience. To yield to either, Leon knew, would make him appear foolish. Thoughtfully he looked at the monk. The Universal Brotherhood could not be assessed by appearances. They had spread to a multitude of worlds and had friends in high places. To antagonise them would be unwise. To appeal to their friendship, even, perhaps, gain their support would be a clever move.

He thumbed the button on his phone. 'Those embroideries,' he said to his social secretary. 'Cancel their purchase. Instead give the credit to a monk of the Universal Brotherhood. I'll give him a note.' Killing the phone, he scribbled a few words on a sheet of paper. 'Here. I have five per cent of my last dividend left. Use it as you will.'

'Brother, you are most generous!'

'Perhaps.' Leon held the man with his eyes. 'Or perhaps I am ambitious,' he said softly. 'It could be that I seek your aid. Another question, Brother. What can you give me in return?'

'Our prayers, brother. Our aid in case of need.'

Leon shrugged. 'Your prayers I can do without, your aid also. Come, man, can't you do better than that?'

Brother Elas rose, held out the order, let it fall to the desk. 'Charity, brother, is the act of giving without asking, a gift without hope of reward,' he said quietly. 'We seek your charity, nothing else.'

'Offering nothing in return?'

'Charity is an act of virtue, brother. Virtue is its own reward.'

Small return for five percent residue of dividend, thought Leon. But how could you argue with a fanatic? The monk could be nothing else. And yet he had to admire the man. At least he lived by his principles. 'Here,' he called as the monk reached the door. 'You have forgotten to take what you came for.' He pushed the order across the desk.

★ ★ ★

Stockholder Mere Evan paced the room, his impatience mounting with every step. A thin film of sweat shone on his ebony features, ran from beneath the crimped wool of his hair, telltale signs of high living which even the air-conditioning could not prevent. He turned as Leon entered, relaxing as he gestured to a table ringed with chairs, all but two occupied. 'At last,' he said. 'What kept you?'

Leon glanced at his watch. 'Am I late?'

'No,' admitted Evan as he took his seat. 'It's just that I thought you would have been more anxious,' he explained. 'After the success of yesterday. Well,' he defended, 'it is a special occasion.'

'Because we won?' Leon stood by his chair, glanced around the room. It was panelled in warm-grained wood polished to a delicate glow, the ceiling a mass of intricate carving, relic of a bygone fashion. 'Has this place been checked for electronic devices?'

'It has.' Restern, the chairman, short, square, laconic, gestured to the man at his side. 'Sheem took care of that. He had also fitted a mechanism that emits a heterodyning barrier. We are safe from spies.'

Perhaps, thought Leon, but are we safe from traitors? It was impossible ever to be sure of that. Touchy pride could seek revenge at any time for an imagined insult. Greed, still the most potent motivation, could lure someone into making a quick profit, fear the same. Sitting down, he looked at each of his fellows. Nine men, ten including himself, the whole of the Spinners Association playing the conspirator. Was it the danger, he wondered, that led them on? The added spice to enliven uneventful living? That was easier to believe than that they were all altruists working together for the common good.

Sheem rose to speak. 'As you all know, the challenge met by the Toymaster has resulted in our gaining yet another block of stock. This will be shared among us as agreed. We now have to consider our next move.'

'Another challenge,' said Evan impulsively.

Sheem raised his eyebrows and looked around the circle of men. 'Any in favour?'

No one moved.

'Any other suggestions?'

Leon resisted the impulse to raise his hand. Let others be in the forefront, he thought. The last thing he wished was to gain a reputation like Evan's. The man spoke too long and too often. Worse, he spoke without thinking. A child, thought Leon. A danger. But the man was a stockholder, a member of the Association. He had to be tolerated.

'I do not think we can repeat another similar wager,' said Restern quietly. 'For one thing, the Toymaster is no fool despite his erratic behaviour. For another, the risk of losing is too great.' He glared at Evan as he tried to interrupt. 'We managed to contract all available fighters of experience to wear our colours. Groshen was reduced to skimming the block, snatching freshly arrived travellers, impressing inexperienced men. Naturally, because of that, he lost. But if we should make a similar wager he will use his personal guards. Do any of you imagine that paid mercenaries could beat that elite corps of men?'

He paused, waiting.

'There are other ways of making and winning wagers,' said Evan. 'We don't necessarily have to put men into the arena. How about challenging him to a personal game? Chess, perhaps, or skag?'

Sheem was cutting. 'Who will play? You?'

Evan hesitated. 'I would if I had the

skill,' he said. 'But . . . '

'Who, then?' Restern, careless of the offence his interruption may have caused, looked around the circle. 'As I thought. No one here is willing to risk the Toymaster's displeasure by an outright attack. I cannot blame you. Even now we cannot tell the repercussions of Stockholder Hurl's victory. Groshen does not like to be beaten. His pride is a tender thing.' He looked at Leon. 'It would be as well for you to allow him to best you in some small matter,' he suggested. 'I apologise for any offence the concept may hold.'

'Your apology is accepted,' said Leon. 'I have already given the matter my attention. A pair of matched slaves who have caught the Toymaster's eye. I will lose them to him when the time is ripe.'

Restern nodded. 'You will not delay too long?'

'No.'

'You are wise. The Association will, naturally, recompense you for your loss.' Again he glanced around the table. 'Suggestions?'

'Let us pool our dividends, hire a band of trained mercenaries, attack the palace and take over.' Mulwo was as impatient and as hotheaded as his ancestors. 'And we won't fight with those stupid swords and spears either. We'll use automatic weapons, lasers, gas even. A hundred worlds are eager to supply what we need.'

'Revolution,' said Restern. 'Armed men, blood in the streets, wanton destruction. And we would have no certainty of winning. You should know what will happen then.'

He knew, thought Leon, watching Mulwo's set features. His maternal grandfather had tried direct rebellion. Of the entire family only his mother had survived and that because she was off-world at the time. It had taken twenty years, half her stock and a new Toymaster before she had been permitted to return.

Mulwo cleared his throat.

'My apologies,' said Restern quickly, 'for any offence my words may have caused.'

'I accept your apology,' growled Mulwo. 'Will you take a vote?'

The vote went against his suggestion

and he sat glowering at the table, a volcano ready to erupt.

'May I suggest attrition?' Another man broke the uneasy silence. 'Subtle but direct influence on the Toymaster? The bending of his will by the use of drugs and suggestion? I have a slave,' he explained. 'A girl, young and lovely, who would be perfect as a weapon. Treated by my technicians she would . . .'

' . . . be spotted the very first time he put a mentaprobe to work on her psyche,' interrupted Restern. 'And that would be before he ever saw her. A good suggestion, Amish,' he said gently. 'But one based on insufficient knowledge.' He looked about the table. 'Anything else?'

'A direct challenge,' said Leon slowly, wishing that the suggestion had come from somebody else. 'It will come sooner or later,' he defended. 'One of us or someone working for us must face the Toymaster and challenge him. The situation is allowed for in Original Law. A Toymaster can be displaced by a majority vote, which is impossible to achieve, or by a direct, personal challenge to prove his mental and physical right to rule this planet. A defence against decadence,' he explained. 'Director Conrad of Grail knew the dangers attending a corporate society and guarded against them in the Certificate of Corporation.'

'True,' mused Restern. 'But such a challenge can only be issued by a stockholder owning ten percent minimum. Who do we know who owns that amount of stock?' Regretfully he shook his head. 'It is one of those impossible dreams, Stockholder Hurl. It could have been done at first, perhaps, but not now. The diversity of stock is too great. Long before we could negotiate even temporary possession of such an amount the Toymaster would strike.'

'Quara,' said Evan suddenly. 'She must own almost the necessary amount.'

'The sister of the Toymaster?' Mulwo snorted his contempt. 'Are you insane? Do you imagine that for one moment she would join us against her brother?'

Evan was stubborn. 'Why not? He dies and she inherits. The prize would be worth her while.'

'And if she loses?'

'Death in torment.' Evan looked around the table. 'But if we all back her how can she lose?'

'Very well, Stockholder Evan, let us assume that.' Sheem put his finger on the glaringly obvious. 'She wins and becomes the new Toymaster. Are we fighting to set a different foot on our throats? The same family,' he pointed out. 'The same blood. The Groshens are not noted for their mercy.' He watched their faces, their disappointment. He spoke before that disappointment could grow, before tempers could fray. 'I suggest we leave all plans to the future. It will give us time to consolidate our winnings and to think not only of the advantages but also the flaws in any plan. Now, Stockholders, let us attend to the normal business of the Spinners Association. Stockholder Sheem?'

Leon sat back, half-listening to the business details, the figures of production, sales, weights, patterns and prices that governed the sale and supply of webs. Another failure, he thought. Another dead end. More delay as the cabal found reasons for not doing what so obviously had to be done.

Of them all Mulwo had produced the only really practical suggestion.

3

Dumarest sighed, stretched, jerked fully awake with the realisation that something was wrong. He cautiously extended his hand, felt for the rifle he had placed beside him, found nothing but the harshness of stone. He turned. The place where he had chosen to sleep was far back in the cave they had selected for a hiding place. From outside birds screamed as they wheeled through the salty air. Sunlight streamed through the opening, thrusting golden spears into the dimness, illuminating the entire area on which the antigrav raft had rested.

It was gone. The cave was empty. The vehicle, Legrain, the rifles, all had vanished. Dumarest rose, eyes narrowed as he searched the uneven floor. He could see no signs of a struggle, no trace of blood. He looked again, then checked the spot where he had lain, felt in his pockets, his boots. He found nothing but his knife. There was no message of any kind.

A pool of water stood to one side against a wall. He knelt, scooped up a double handful, laved his face and neck. Cautiously he sipped some of the liquid; it was loaded with brine, undrinkable. Rising, he walked to the edge of the cave and stared thoughtfully outside.

He saw nothing but the wheeling birds, the eye-bright orb of the sun. It hung low in the sky, almost touching the horizon. He had slept for a long time; the dryness of his mouth and the hunger in his stomach confirmed this. Soon it would be night. Then would come the freezing wind, ice-spray carried from the sea, the rapid fall in temperature. From a haven the cave had turned into a trap.

He edged closer to the opening. A clump of vegetation offered a handhold. He grasped it, tugged, made certain that it would hold his weight. Gripping it, he leaned far out and looked below, staring at the rocks, the spuming waves. He twisted his head to look up at a vertical wall of grey stone blotched with the chalky droppings of birds.

It was weathered, eroded, the surface

flawed so that an agile man would have a chance to climb to the summit. Against that were the wind, the slippery surface, the wheeling birds whose guano crusted every niche — birds who would attack any menace to their nests. And a fall would mean certain death on the rocks below. To remain in the cave without food, water or fire held a predictable outcome.

Dumarest had no choice but to climb.

Easing himself back into the cave, he sipped a little of the brackish water, again laved his face and neck, cleansed his hands of dirt and grime. Clamping his teeth on the blade of his knife, he returned to the mouth of the cave, gripped the clump of vegetation and swung himself through the opening. Left hand holding tight to the sparse growth, left foot still on the ledge of the cave, he sought for hand and toeholds for his right hand and foot. He found them, muscles straining as he pulled himself up and away from the mouth of the cave. Slowly, spider-like, he crawled up the vertical wall. The wind pressed against his back like a giant hand.

His fingers brushed twigs, the structure of a nest perched on a ledge. He moved his hand, pushed aside the obstruction, clamped fingers on the smeared surface. A bird screamed and flung itself at his back. The blow was hard, punishing, only the metal mesh buried in the grey plastic saving him from the vicious beak. Its neck broken, the creature fell, its place immediately taken by its mate. Dumarest released his right hand, snatched the knife from his mouth, slashed as the bird lunged towards his eyes. Feathers spun in the sunlight as the headless creature plummeted to the sea. Grimly Dumarest continued to climb.

A ledge gave him a respite. He rested, chest heaving, uneasily conscious of his physical limitations. He had done too much too soon. The exertion of the battle, the strain of running, hiding, the fight against the cold and darkness, the capture of the raft and the long, tedious flight over the sea. All with scarcely any sleep or food. For any man it would have been an ordeal, but they had taken him fresh from travelling Low, his body-fat depleted, his reserves of energy at a minimum.

Rising, he peered up at the cliff, searching for handholds, a way to the top. A thin, jagged crack ran diagonally from the ledge, promising a relatively easy path. Teeth clamped on knife, he thrust his hands into the narrow opening, boots scrabbling as they searched for a hold so as to relieve the strain. Inch by inch he moved up and away from the ledge, conscious only of the rock before his eyes, the wind at his back, the dragging ache of his muscles.

The crack narrowed, petered out; beyond was nothing but sheer, polished stone. Dumarest reared back, looking directly overhead. The wind gusted from the cliff, came between his body and the rock, threatened to push him from his precarious hold. Sweating, he forced himself closer to the stone. He had seen a streak of darkness above, a thin fissure revealed by the light of the setting sun.

He gripped his knife, aimed, drove the point hard in the crack. It was narrow, too close to penetrate with a finger, but it accepted the blade of the knife. He pounded it home with his fist, gripped the hilt, pulled on it as he lifted his weight, left hand searching for purchase. He found it, muscles turning into iron beneath the necessity to grip or fall. A foot fitted into the hold relinquished by his right hand. Another into the one vacated by his left. Releasing his grip on the knife Dumarest reached out, felt despair as his fingers met smooth stone, desperation as they touched a rough edge. Touched but could not grip.

Carefully he lifted his right foot, rested it on the knife, prayed that it would hold. A surge and he had risen, total weight balanced on the blade, right hand reaching, gripping, the fingers turning into steel claws as the blade snapped beneath his weight. Suspended by one hand, he hung against the cliff, arm and shoulder muscles dull with pain. Then his left hand found a hold, then his boots, and with the strength of desperation he was up and away from the danger point.

Above there now remained only a

crumbling slope thick with vegetation, scarred and fissured by the forces which sought constantly to topple the summit of the cliff into the sea. Dumarest crawled up it, reached the top, pulled himself over. Ten steps from the edge he stumbled and fell, grass and sky whirling as he fought the nausea of exhaustion, the gusting wind merging with the roar of blood in his ears.

'Get up!' The voice came from above and behind, deep and strong yet feminine. 'You there! Get up on your feet!'

Dumarest rolled, looked to where a raft floated just above the ground. A woman stared at him from the pilot's seat. She wore a sleeved tunic of brilliant yellow embroidered with a pattern of scarlet. A short cloak of similar design hung from her shoulders. Her face was dark, lined with age and experience, the crinkled hair tight against her skull. Her eyes were deep-set, hard. Her mouth and jaw were those of a man. Jewels gleamed from the lobes of her ears.

'My lady?' Dumarest fought for time, for breath, for energy. This was a member of the ruling class of Toy. His eyes left the mannish face at the sound of bells and laughter.

Behind the woman stood two children, their skin-colour a delicate olive. They were dressed in red and yellow, the garments all of one piece, the colours in a checkerboard design. Snug hoods rimmed their faces. Crest-like protrusions carried tiny bells, their sounds ornamenting the wind. In the dying sunlight they resembled dancing flames as they balanced on the rail, jumping, moving, never still.

'You had better do as Stockholder Ledra says,' said one.

'That's right,' echoed the other. 'Get up on your feet while you still have the chance.'

Their voices were incongruous. Not children, thought Dumarest, studying their faces as he rose and approached the raft. Small people. Men less than two feet tall but perfectly proportioned. The fruits, he guessed, of biological engineering. A strain bred for smallness to be used as novelties, toys, pets, amusing additions to a wealthy household.

He looked at the woman. 'My lady,' he said, 'I beg your charity. I need assistance. Food, water, transportation to the city. I was dumped,' he explained. 'Left in a cave to starve or freeze. I had to climb up the cliff to escape.'

One of the little men whistled. 'Dumped? In a cave?'

Dumarest nodded.

'What did you do?' The other was eager. 'Sleep with the wrong woman? Win from the wrong man?' The small face looked wise and somehow cunning. 'You can tell us,' he urged. 'We know what goes on in the city.'

'We certainly do,' said the other. He winked at Dumarest. 'It's all in our education,' he explained. 'To command a good price we have to be versatile. Very versatile.' The wink turned into a leer. 'You'd be surprised how many women have a use for a surrogate son. Mother love,' he said. 'I could tell you things about that.'

'Be silent!' snapped the woman. 'Be seated! Remain still!' She looked at Dumarest. 'Excessive development of the

60

thyroid,' she explained. 'It burns them out but makes them tireless playthings. Sometimes they irritate but are conditioned to obey a certain tone of voice. You understand?'

'Yes, my lady.' Dumarest glanced to the rear of the raft. The two manikins sat perfectly still, apparently asleep, their eyes closed, faces lax,

'So you were dumped,' said Ledra thoughtfully. 'Such a thing is unusual on Toy. Killed, crippled, tormented, yes, but never before have I heard of a man being taken to a place of jeopardy and there abandoned. Their names?'

'I do not know, my lady. They were masked. Paid bravos, no doubt.'

'No doubt,' she said dryly, and then, 'I saw you climb the cliff. The latter part at least. You must have great courage and stamina. They are qualities I can use.'

Dumarest was cautious. 'My lady?'

'I am the Stockholder Ledra. On Toy this is both title and respectful form of address.'

'My apologies, Stockholder Ledra.'

'The title is sufficient. Well?' She

recognised his bewilderment. 'I am offering you a bargain. Medical attention that you so obviously need in return for a supply of your germ plasm. Your genes bear certain characteristics that I may find of use. I am a biological engineer,' she explained. 'Among other things I am attempting to breed a strain of warrior-guards. Courage and stamina are two qualities they must naturally possess. If you agree to the bargain, get into the raft.'

* ★ *

It was almost dark when they reached the factory. The sun had lowered itself beneath the horizon and already the heat of the day was streaming into space, untrapped by the almost total lack of carbon dioxide in the atmosphere. Lights shone on the large, flat roof of the main building. A section slid aside, closing behind them as the raft settled. A white-coated attendant came forward as Ledra stepped from the vehicle.

'Success, Stockholder?'

'Failure.' The hard, mannish face was

in direct contrast to that of the young girl assistant. 'The bone structure is still far too heavy. We must reduce the size even more and risk the loss of intelligence. I think the wingspan is as large as can be managed but the legs could be sacrificed if necessary.'

'That would be a wide divergence from the initial specifications, Stockholder.'

'True, but we may have to compromise. An experiment,' said Ledra, turning to Dumarest. 'An attempt to manufacture a flying man. I was testing the latest result just before I found you. The wind was too strong. The creature was unable to control its wings.'

'And, Stockholder?'

'It fell into the sea.' She snapped brisk orders at the attendant. 'Wake those two manikins. Give them both two minutes of punishment at level eight. They must learn to control their tongues. Impertinence is not a saleable commodity.'

'As you order, Stockholder.'

'Flush the vat containing experiment eighty-three. We shall have to start from scratch. When you have finished report to me in the laboratory.' Ledra turned to Dumarest as the girl walked away. 'Do you find her attractive?'

'She is pleasing to look at, Stockholder.'

'You are cautious,' said the woman. 'Another desirable trait.' She rested the white palm of her hand on his forehead, his wrist. 'You are close to exhaustion. We had best waste no more time.'

Dumarest followed her down a corridor, past a series of cages in which crouched shadowed figures, through a door and into a place of machines and sterile brilliance. An oddly shaped chair stood beside a tall cabinet studded with dials and buttons.

'Strip, and wash,' ordered Ledra. 'There is a shower through that door. Leave your clothes. They will be cleaned and returned.'

The water was hot, comforting, helping to ease the pain of bruised flesh and overstrained muscles. Dumarest took his time, washing his hair, his body, enjoying the impact of the spray, taking advantage of the opportunity to think. It was hard.

His body was poisoned with too great an accumulation of toxins. Any great physical exertion now would throw him into a coma in which he would hover on the edge of death. There was nothing he could do but take full advantage of the present opportunity to regain his strength.

He stood naked before a drier, the hot air helping to relax him even more. He returned naked to the laboratory where the woman waited.

'Stand here.' She weighed him, stared at him as if he were another specimen she was about to dissect. 'Thin,' she commented. 'Too thin. Where did you get all those bruises?'

'The men who took me to the cave, Stockholder,' he said. 'They were not gentle.'

She shrugged, not commenting on the lie. 'Sit down,' she commanded. 'Drink this.'

She handed him a pint of warm, thick fluid. Cautiously, he tasted it. Like basic, he thought. Sickly with glucose, loaded with protein, laced with vitamins. A cupful contained enough energy to keep a spaceman alive for a day. Gratefully he swallowed the contents of the beaker.

'And this.' She refilled the container. 'That will give your stomach something to work on,' she explained. 'You know, the human digestive system is remarkably rugged and efficient. You eat food, it is processed in the stomach, certain essences removed, the rest evicted. But that takes time. By eliminating the processing we can save that time.' She reached out, took the empty container from his hand. 'Now lie back and relax.'

He watched as she brooded over the panel.

'The most efficient way to get you into full physical condition would be to use slow time,' she mused. 'Accelerate your metabolism up to a ratio of forty-to-one, feed you intravenously, keep you unconscious with drugs. You know of slow time?'

'Yes, Stockholder.'

'You would. Travellers usually do. Quick time also, no doubt?'

'It is used on a High passage,' he said, wondering what she was getting at. 'It shortens the apparent time of the journey

66

by slowing the metabolism and altering the time-sense. An hour becomes a minute.'

'Exactly, but I intend to use neither. There is a better method.' She deftly inserted hollow needles into his arm. Tubes led from them to the cabinet. Dials clicked as she pressed buttons. 'As I suspected, a dangerously high toxic level.' More buttons sank beneath her finger, then she turned to look at Dumarest. 'Your blood is being processed through this machine. It will determine the optimum constitution and remove all fatigue-inducing toxic elements. It will also add a stream of easily assimilated concentrates to restore your physical energy. In effect, you are now in the position of a man who is both asleep and eating great quantities of highly nutritious food.'

Uneasily he wondered what else was being added to his blood. Hypnotic agents? Truth serums? It was obvious that the woman hadn't believed his story. Even now she could be rendering him helpless for later collection by the authorities. He forced himself to be calm — there was nothing he could do about it. Nothing but be polite. 'Thank you, Stockholder,' he said.

She shrugged. 'We made a bargain. When you are fit I shall collect my share of it.' She looked up as the door opened. Heels rapped across the floor and the girl who had met the raft stood beside the chair. 'Have you done as ordered?'

'Yes, Stockholder.'

'Good.' The woman turned, a swirl of yellow and scarlet against the sterile whiteness of the laboratory. 'I am fatigued. Stay here with the man. When I am rested we shall collect his germ plasm.'

*　*　*

Time, thought Dumarest. *How much time? How long dare I wait?* He opened his eyes and looked at the girl. She sat on a chair at his side, reading, unaware of his examination. Dumarest maintained the regularity of his breathing. It hadn't been hard to counterfeit sleep; the difficulty had been in staying awake. Despite the machine processing his blood the warmth and comfort had done their work. That and the silence broken only by the sound of breathing, the rustle of a turned page.

Hard, he thought, studying the girl's profile. The mouth and jaw bore a resemblance to the stockholder's. Still young, still attractive, she would harden into masculinity with the passage of years. To appeal to her sympathy would be a waste of time; people who manufactured monsters could have none of the soft, human emotions. And why should she help a man who had killed those of her own kind?

Carefully Dumarest moved his right arm, the fingers reaching toward the needles embedded in his left, clamping about the tubes, squeezing them shut He would lose, he guessed, about half a pint of blood if he tore them free, maybe a little more. It was a loss he had to stand. At any moment the machine could add some sleep-inducing drug to his blood-stream. It was logical to assume that it would. Logical to assume that it hadn't done so yet because it was still working to remove present toxins. But why hadn't they used restraints?

Psychology, he thought. A trick to keep him calm and amenable. That or a sublime arrogance that precluded the concept that he would dare to escape, to do other than what the stockholder desired. But, even so, she had left the girl as a watchdog.

A lamp flashed on the cabinet and a warning device gave a harsh buzz. The girl looked up, rose, spun toward Dumarest as he tore the needles from his arm. Before she could scream his hand was on her throat, fingers pressing hard against the carotid arteries. She slumped unconscious; gently he eased her to the floor.

Pulsing blood welled from the wounds left by the needles. He stooped, ripped fabric from the girl's dress, bound it tightly about his arm. His clothes lay where he had left them, still uncleaned.

He dressed and returned to the laboratory. The warning device still emitted its harsh noise. He pressed a button beneath the flashing light and both light and buzzer died. In the following silence footsteps echoed from the corridor outside.

Dumarest crossed the laboratory, passing enigmatic machines, electronic microscopes, meson probes, dispensers holding a thousand chemicals, the working tools of a biological engineer. He crouched behind the door, waiting, hands stiffened to chop and stab. The footsteps grew louder, came level, diminished as they continued down the corridor. A patrolling guard, he thought; the footsteps had carried the regular, mechanical beat of such a person. There would be others and with good reason. Stockholder Ledra would have no desire to be surprised by an attack of the monsters she had created.

Outside, the passage had a faint, acrid smell, the taint of chemicals and caged beasts. A faint mewing came from further down where the cages ran from floor to roof, a stinging and a strange rattle as of claws on steel. Beyond lay the landing stage beneath the roof, the raft, a way to the open air. Dumarest ran toward it, freezing as light blazed at the end of the corridor, the harsh glare reflecting from the polished floor.

Creatures muttered in the cages, crying out as the light seared their eyes. A group of men surrounding the light halted, staring at what it showed. 'Incredible!'

A thin falsetto echoed above the cries. 'See, Amrush? A cunning blend of bird, man and reptile. Note the clawed feet, the scales, the crest of feathers. How, I wonder, would a pair of these mate?'

'Buy me, Stockholder,' said a thick, drooling voice. 'Buy me and find out.'

'And this.' The light moved closer to where Dumarest hugged the wall. 'Amazing. Have you ever seen such a plethora of feminine charms? Such a one would be worth an entire harem of ordinary slaves. Think of the combinations, the permutations.'

'It would kill you with loving,' said another of the group. 'But have we come to see such as these? Where are the manikins?'

'In a lower chamber, Gentles,' said the man who carried the light. An attendant, thought Dumarest. A guide. A salesman whose task it was to display the wares of the factory. 'Men and women both, Gentles. Young, virile and highly trained in amusing arts. If you will follow me I shall be honoured to display their prowess.'

Dumarest turned as the light grew brighter, ducked through a door, found it gave onto a flight of stairs leading down. He followed it, another, two more. He must now be at ground level, he thought, or even lower. The air held a musty, dank smell despite the soft breeze from the air-conditioners. A passage led into darkness, water splashing at the far end. He hesitated, then, as sounds echoed from above, ran down the corridor.

Halfway along something grabbed him by the ankle.

He fell twisting so as to land on his shoulders, kicking out with his free foot, feeling something yield beneath the impact of his boot. Water splashed and a faint green phosphorescence illuminated the area. In the dull light Dumarest could see an amorphous shape floating in a tank of water, a naked skull in which shone blue eyes, a fringe of tentacles, a lipped mouth from which came bubbling words. 'Come, my pretty. Come to me. Share my home.'

He slashed with the edge of his stiffened hand as a tentacle reached for his throat. Another wound around his waist, tightening, dragging him to the edge of the water. Desperately he leaned forward, thumbs stabbing at the shining blue eyes. The thing screamed, threw him backward, threshed the water into foam.

'Cruel!' it blubbered. 'Cruel to treat me so!'

Sickened, Dumarest climbed to his feet, raced down the passage. A woman, he thought. The thing had once been a woman or a scrap of germ plasm which would have grown into a girl had not the biological engineer interfered. She had cut, altered, adapted, grafted a new gene pattern, stimulated with chemicals, treated with forced growth under the impetus of slow time. Created a freak for the titivation of her fellows. A pathetic thing destined to provide a momentary amusement. On Toy not only the weather was cruel.

The passage ended in a steel door dogged fast but unlocked. He dragged it open, found stairs, raced upward. A face gaped at him from a landing. He struck out, felt cartilage yield beneath his fist, ran on. Behind him came shouts, cries, the thud of running feet. The stairs ended at another door. He tore it open, passed through, shut and bolted the panel. Beyond lay the landing stage, rafts, the controls governing the sliding panel in the roof. An attendant turned, stiffened as Dumarest clamped his hands around his throat.

'Open the roof,' he snapped. 'Quick!'

The attendant gurgled, reached for a lever. Night air streamed through the opening panel, frigid, numbing with cold. Dumarest clubbed the man senseless and ran toward the rafts. One rested directly beneath the opening, a covered vehicle, probably used by the visiting party. He dragged back the canopy, climbed inside, flung himself at the controls. Engines whined to life, fans blasting the almost weightless raft upward, sending it forward as he cleared the roof. Slamming shut the canopy, he advanced the forward speed and searched for the heater control. Turning it full on he sagged back in the pilot's seat.

Free, he thought, *but for how long*? Within seconds they would be after him in the remaining rafts. Messages would be sent ahead to watch for his vehicle. Patrol ships would be watching to blast him from the sky.

Irritably he shook his head. It was the reaction, the sudden cessation of effort, the effect of accumulated toxins in his blood. The rapid action had once again depleted his reserves, that and the savage chill of the night. Shivering, he tried to turn the heater control even higher.

For the moment he was safe. Lightless, the raft could not be spotted at night and, by the dawn, he should be well away from the factory, with luck safely hidden in the city. Leaning back, he stared at the stars visible through the transparent canopy. About midnight, he guessed. Say another six or seven hours to dawn. Long enough for him to reach the city, leave the raft, proceed on foot. Long enough, even, to catch a few hours of sleep.

The thought was tempting; resolutely he pushed it away. A sleeping man was helpless to avoid the most trivial danger and he had to stay awake to guide the raft, find a landing place, merge with the life of the city.

Again he looked at the stars, checking his position, wondering a little at the distant points of light, the worlds circling those suns. Which was Gath? Which was Folgone? Folgone where Derai lay in a thousand-year subjective sleep. Long gone now, of course, but it would be nice to know where she rested. Folgone and Hive and Gath, a hundred remembered worlds.

But, above all, which was Earth?

4

Battle had been done on a table, men attacking, falling, swept aside to lie in careless disarray. The survivors stood, cold and silent, glowing with the colours of ruby and emerald, the board on which they stood fashioned of diamond and jet.

Groshen, Master of Toy, took a sip of wine and frowned as he considered his next move. Three consecutive times he had been beaten and now it had become a matter of pride. To Creel it was child's play, a means to while away an idle hour, an opportunity to educate the ruler of Toy.

'Check.' Groshen moved a piece.

The cyber moved a knight, captured a pawn. 'Checkmate.'

'Again? But how . . . ?' The Toymaster fell silent as he examined the board. Irritably he gulped his wine. 'I thought I had you,' he said petulantly. 'I would have wagered a thousand units of stock on the outcome.'

'It is a matter of prediction,' said Creel evenly. His voice was an inoffensive modulation. 'I have been trained in such matters. With respect, my lord, you have not.'

'I have been trained to rule!'

'That is true, my lord. My ability is nothing against yours but, even so, it has some use. If you will remember I predicted when you moved your first piece that I would checkmate you in seventeen moves. As a matter of curiosity, if you should wish to play again, move as you will and give me the number of moves at the end of which I must have you in checkmate. Any number above seven.'

Groshen puckered his lips. 'You are confident, cyber.'

'Certain, my lord.'

'It is a trick.' Absently the Toymaster set up the pieces, ringed fingers flashing in the light. He was a man of early middle age, tall, in superb condition, his thick neck corded with muscle. His eyes held a peculiar brilliance and he had a mannerism of inhaling through his mouth and exhaling through his nose. 'You are trying to prove something.'

Creel made no attempt to deny the accusation. 'That is true, my lord. I am attempting to prove to you the worth of the service offered by the Cyclan. Many rulers are pleased to retain a cyber.'

'To influence their decisions?'

'To advise, my lord. Nothing more. To tell you the logical outcome of any proposed action. To help you arrive at a decision by presenting you with the inevitable result of any sequence of events.'

'At a price,' said Groshen shrewdly. 'The maintenance of yourself and your acolytes. A heavy sum paid to the Cyclan. Why should I pay for what I already possess?'

'A cyber, my lord?'

'The Library.' Groshen leaned back in his ornate chair. It reflected the barbaric leanings of the rulers of Toy as did the sumptuous furnishings of the room. The hangings were of the finest weave, blazing with colour, each tapestry depicting an event in the history of Toy. The floor was tesselated with slabs of precious metal. Even the guards, each seven feet tall, armed with ceremonial sword and shield, were dressed in cloth of silver. The Toymaster himself wore white and gold, his dark skin in startling contrast to the snowy fabric. 'The Library,' he repeated. 'As I told you, cyber, Toy owns a computer. A very large and very efficient machine. With it I can predict all I wish to know.'

'Everything, my lord?'

'All I need to know,' Groshen repeated testily. 'Can any man or machine predict everything in the universe? To do so they would need to know all that can be known. An apparent impossibility.' He helped himself to more wine. 'So you see, cyber, you waste your time, Toy has no need of the services of the Cyclan.'

Creel picked up a chessman, placed it on a square, picked up another. In his scarlet robe he looked like a living flame, the Cyclan seal glinting on his breast as he moved, his shaved skull death-like above the thrown-back cowl. 'You have probably asked the Library to predict the future demand for pattern one-five-three of the factory belonging to Stockholder Hurl. Am I correct, my lord?'

'How should I know? These details are not of my concern.' Groshen narrowed his eyes. 'You are after something, cyber. Very well. Let us find out what you want to know.' He lifted a communicator, spoke into the instrument. 'Library. What is the sales prediction on pattern one-five-three, Hurl?' He raised the amplification.

'The prediction is that an extra fifty percent will be sold this month, Toymaster,' said a thin voice.

'And after?'

'One hundred percent for the next three.'

Groshen smiled at the cyber. 'Well?'

'The machine is wrong, my lord. My advice is to discontinue that pattern for at least six months. A singer is becoming prominent on Artus,' he explained. 'That world is your biggest customer for that particular design.'

'So?'

'The woman's name is Melange. It is

the name of a flower and it has become a fad on Artus. The design of one-five-three is that of a bird. A bird, my lord, is not a flower.'

Groshen spoke into the communicator. 'Listen to this.'

'The buyers from Artus will want designs incorporating the flower melange. I would suggest that Stockholder Hurl concentrate on pattern six-three-two and also pattern five-four-nine. Both have a melange as their central theme.'

'A transient fashion, Toymaster,' said the voice from the communicator.

'If a fashion cannot be created then it must be followed,' snapped Groshen. 'Incorporate the information and issue as necessary. And, Vohmis, one more such error and I shall have you arraigned for inefficiency.' Scowling, he slammed down the instrument.

Creel was quick to salve his wounded pride. 'The Library is a machine, my lord. It can only base its predictions on information already in its memory banks. It can only extrapolate from known data. The Cyclan does not work with such limited tools. A cyber must consider the effect of intangibles, influences, latent desires, unsuspected directives.'

'The Library was founded by my ancestors,' said the Toymaster curtly. 'It has been added to over the centuries. It is the largest instrument of its kind in this sector of the galaxy — perhaps even the largest there is. On it rests the wealth of Toy. Not only for its predictions governing production and trade, but as an instrument for hire. And,' he added viciously, 'it is impersonal. It owes allegiance to no group or clan. Can you, cyber, say the same?'

Creel remained silent. Only the shifting gleam of the seal on his breast betraying a sign of life.

Groshen rose, crossed to a window, the polarised glass clearing as he touched a control. Outside shone the stars, the glimmering nightlights of the city. From the landing field came a cold glare of brilliance. There, men heavily muffled against the cold sweated as they loaded cargo into the holds of waiting spaceships.

The Toymaster scowled. He hated the night, the cold, the mystery of darkness. To him the stars were alien eyes peering down at his domain, the darkness a cloak for intrigue and subterfuge. What were they planning now? he wondered. Safe in the darkness, faceless shapes of menace, shadows aligned against his will. He squinted down into the courtyard beneath the window. Irritably he snatched up the communicator.

'Courtyard,' he snapped. 'Give me light.'

Immediately the area was bathed in the glare of floodlights. Stark in their brilliance hung the bodies of three men. They were naked, wrists lashed to a crossbar, ice forming a pool at their feet.

'Look,' ordered the Toymaster. He waited until the cyber stood at his side. 'Those men are guards. One coughed while on duty, another moved, the third followed my sister with his eyes. If they live through the night they will not again be so careless.' He spoke into the communicator. 'Water,' he commanded. 'Hot. Immediately.'

Gloating, he watched as men came forward with hoses. Vapour rose as they bathed the men with near-boiling water, melting the ice at their feet, the frost from their bodies.

A child, thought Creel dispassionately. A spoiled, vicious child, venting his anger on those helpless to defend themselves.

'A small mind,' said a voice from behind the watchers. 'Only my brother could find amusement in a thing so trivial.'

'Quara!' The Toymaster turned, eyes glinting with anger.

'Yes, my brother. Aren't you glad to see me?'

She was tall, magnificent in her carriage, large-breasted, wide-hipped, full lips betraying her sensuous nature. She wore green, the gown hugging her body, sandals mere strips of leather on her naked feet. Emeralds glinted in the crimped hair. Crushed jade sparkled from the nails of fingers and toes. She wore a poniard in a narrow belt of flexible green metal.

Smiling at the Toymaster, she reached

forward, took the communicator from his hand, spoke into it. 'Release those men. Tend them. The Stockholder Quara Groshen speaks.'

'You go too far, sister!'

'How far is too far, brother?' She looked at him and shook her head. 'Will you never learn? A guard is but a man. He can hate and love and fear as other men. He can brood and nurse a desire for revenge. Our father would never have treated men so. To kill, yes. To torment, never.' She set down the communicator. 'You are but human, brother. Your skin is no thicker than that of any other. A knife, the beam of a laser, poison, a microbe in the air, all can kill you as easily as your meanest slave.'

'I am the Toymaster!'

'You are the largest stockholder on Toy,' she corrected evenly. 'Lose that stock and what do you have? Certainly not the protection of those who love you.'

For a moment Creel thought that she had gone too far. Groshen's eyes reddened, the whites becoming bloodshot with suppressed fury. The bony skin dulled, drained of blood. The lips thinned to an invisible line. And then, incredibly, he laughed.

'You jest, sister. You tease. You do your best but you cannot hide your envy. It is foolish for me to become annoyed.' He lifted his goblet, sipped a little wine. 'Fate, sister. The irony which determined that I was the first-born, you the second. To me the stock and the rule of Toy. To you nothing but the crumbs from the table.'

It was her turn to display rage. Watching, Creel sensed the tension, the boiling anger barely controlled. She turned and he met the impact of her eyes. 'My lady?'

'Leave us!'

'Stay!' Groshen was quick to assert his authority. 'This is my palace, sister. Here I give the orders, not you. Here,' he added significantly, 'and everywhere else on Toy. I advise you never to forget that.'

She bowed, hiding her eyes, hating him and hating the cyber for having witnessed her humiliation. She was too much of a woman to like the robot-like thing of flesh and blood. He was devoid of all emotion. He could not be manipulated like other men. A cyber never knew the meaning of hate and love, envy and fear. An operation performed at puberty divorced the thalamus from the rest of the cortex. The result was a living machine, which could not be bought or coerced. His only loyalty was to the Cyclan, his only possible pleasure the stimulation of mental achievement.

'My lord.' Creel bowed to the Toymaster. It was, he knew, time for him to leave. A cyber always did his best to avoid personal involvement. 'With your permission, my lord. There are things which require my attention.'

'On Toy?'

'Personal matters, my lord.'

Groshen nodded, watched the tall, thin, scarlet figure move toward the door. Beside him Quara gave a low expression of disgust. 'That thing!' she said. 'Why do you tolerate his presence?'

'He has his uses,' said the Toymaster mildly.

'We don't need him.' Quara looked at her brother. 'What uses?'

'He is a clever man,' said Groshen obliquely. 'I am beginning to realise why a ruler needs someone like him.' He crossed to where the chessmen stood on their board. He sat, fingers absently toying with the pieces. 'Not that he has told me anything I did not already suspect,' he added. 'But sometimes it is as well to have confirmation.'

'You talk in riddles, brother.' She moved so as to stand at his side. 'What do you mean?'

'You do not know?' His fingers touched the pieces one after the other. 'Amish,' he said. 'Mulwo, Restern, Hurl, Sheem, Evan, the rest of the Spinners Association. They play a game, my sister. Perhaps you know of it?' He didn't wait for an answer. 'A dangerous game similar to this. Perhaps you have been tempted to aid them; if so accept my advice. No matter what they do they cannot harm the king.' His fingers touched the king and queen. 'The Toymaster. They can put him in check but that is all. But you, the queen, that piece they can sweep from the board.' His hand moved, spilling the pieces, sending them to the carpeted floor. 'Be warned, my sister.'

She stooped, picked up the pieces, not bothering to remind him that life was not a game of chess.

★   ★   ★

On Toy the nights were coldest just before dawn. Then ice glittered in the streets and frost masked closed windows; few were in the streets and those that were hurried to places of warmth and comfort. Muffled, a shapeless bundle in heavy furs, Quara was certain that she had not been followed. Even so she was cautious. Three times she passed the door that was her destination, waiting, listening for footsteps. Within her muff her hand was tight on the butt of a laser, small, silent, deadly. Only when she was convinced that she was unobserved did she halt at the door and press the button in a series of pulses. It opened. She stepped inside, heard the panel close behind her, blinked in a gush of sudden light.

'Stockholder Groshen!' Leon Hurl

stared at her. He was fully dressed, in the middle of his second period of activity. Not even after hundreds of years had the human metabolism managed to adjust itself to the thirty-hour day, the fifteen-hour night. Men worked and slept much after the old pattern. 'Is this wise?'

'I think so.' Swiftly she shed her furs, tucked away her weapon, shivered to the memory of outside cold. 'Is this how you greet me, Leon? No hot spiced tea?'

'My apologies, Stockholder. I am remiss. If you will follow me to the solar I shall attend to your needs.'

'Please, Leon.' Her hand rested familiarly on his arm as he led the way to a room whose roof blazed with sun lamps. 'Must you be so formal? Haven't you known me long enough to talk as a friend?'

'Again I apologise.' He turned, looked at her, eyes soft with memory. A long time, he thought. Long enough to have played with her when she was a child. To give her rides on his shoulders. To dangle her on his knee. How much like her mother she looked! He felt the old pain, the hopeless yearning still undulled by time. Estar was dead now, ashes with her husband, but she lived again in her daughter.

He ushered her into a chair, went to order tea, carrying it himself to shield her from the curious eyes of the household slaves.

She sipped, looked at him across the vapour rising from the cup. 'The Toymaster,' she said abruptly. 'He knows.'

He looked at his hand. The liquid in his cup remained still. Well, he thought, it had to come sooner or later. Ten men could not hold a secret for long. But did he just suspect or did he have proof? And, if so, could the girl be involved? He sipped, thinking. It was unlikely. She met none of the cabal aside from himself and they always exercised the greatest caution.

'Leon!' She was disturbed at his silence. 'Don't you understand? He knows!'

'He probably does,' he admitted. 'But what does he know? That we of the Spinners Association have combined to obtain more stock in a variety of ways?

That is not against the regulations. It isn't contrary to Original Law. Does he guess at your part in all this?'

'I'm not sure,' she said. 'I think so. He spoke oddly and warned me not to be involved. It could have been an empty threat or more of the workings of his twisted mind. Leon! What shall we do?'

He poured himself more tea. 'Nothing.'

'But . . . '

'What can he really know? That we meet and talk and that is all.' But, he reminded himself, some of the talk had been less than wise. Mulwo with his suggestion to hire mercenaries and stage an armed rebellion. That alone would be enough to incriminate them all. Who could be the traitor? he wondered. Restern? Evan? How to tell among so many? 'Tell me,' he said quietly, 'did the Toymaster name names? State facts?'

'Names, yes. Facts, no.'

'Then it could all be surmise,' he pointed out. 'A desire to claim greater knowledge than he has. With respect, Quara, your brother is not wholly sane. Such a man would be suspicious of a shadow. Did he say anything else?' he urged. 'Give a source of information, perhaps?'

Slowly she shook her head, then, 'The cyber! He claimed that Creel had his uses, that a ruler would be wise to have such a one at his side.' She frowned. 'What could he know? A stranger to Toy.'

'Do not underestimate the Cyclan,' said Leon sombrely. 'The red swine are clever. From two facts a cyber can make a third, more. A hint and he will predict the logical development of events. And, for some reason, he wants to gain the favour of the Toymaster. Do you know why?'

Quara shook her head.

'It could be important,' mused Leon. 'The Cyclan does nothing without reason. I wish that I knew.'

'The meeting,' she said. 'What was discussed? Did you make any resolutions?'

'Nothing of importance. Just to postpone any future action. It was the usual thing,' he explained. 'Mulwo wanted to stage an armed rebellion but lacked any support. Amish suggested eroding the Toymaster by planting an instrument

95

pliant to our will. Evan . . . ' He broke off.

'Well?'

'He made a wild suggestion,' he said carefully. 'He could not know of your interest.'

'Tell me.'

'I mentioned the possibility of challenging the Toymaster as provided for in the Original Laws but, as Restern pointed out, it is an impossible dream. The challenger has to hold at least ten percent of stock to become eligible. Evan mentioned your name. He pointed out that you hold the necessary amount.'

He fell silent, not looking at her, hearing the faint exhalation of her breath.

'A challenge,' she said thoughtfully. 'I hadn't thought of that.'

'The risk is too great,' he said quickly. 'If you lose you will be ruined and perhaps worse. And you will lose. The place, style and choice of weapons reside in the control of the Toymaster. It would be impossible to best him.' He looked down at his hand. The fingers were curved to reflect his thoughts. 'He has us,' he said. 'In the hollow of his hand. All we can do is sit and wait for him to move against us.'

'And while you wait he will ruin the planet.' She rose, paced the floor, eyes blazing with the memory of past humiliations. 'Already we are a mockery to more cultured worlds. Slaves! Battles! The iron grip of tyranny! Our ancestors did not plan for this, Leon! Somehow he has to be stopped!'

True, he thought tiredly. But when, how and by whom?

★ ★ ★

Feet soundless on the thick carpets, Creel strode through the corridors of the palace towards the rooms which had been placed at his disposal. Even as he walked his mind evaluated the data around him. The guards, magnificent examples of humanity, stood in alcoves, living statues of flesh, bone and muscle, yet their eyes were dulled, betraying their lack of intelligence. Tapestries livened the darkest corner with boasting colours, carving adorned every

97

surface. Even the air held the taint of incense.

Barbarians, he thought. Children displaying their love of garish colour, easily amused, violent in their passions, thoughtlessly cruel. Not a decadent society but one that had flowered in its own fashion, unchecked by the influence of older worlds. But here, he thought, motives were transparently obvious: greed, desire, the struggle for personal power, hate and fear coupled to envy. Trusted tools with which to work. It should not be hard to gain a foothold on Toy.

One of his retinue stood outside the door to his private chambers. A young man, sternly impassive, fanatically dedicated to the service of his master. He stiffened as Creel approached, deferentially opened the door.

'You appear fatigued,' said Creel, halting. A tired brain was an inefficient one. 'Your relief?'

'Due in thirty minutes, master.'

'Relay my instructions. Total seal. No interruptions for any reason.' Creel's voice retained its modulation. There was no need for aural emphasis.

Within his private room he crossed to the window, cleared it, frowned at the external layer of frost. Either the heating elements were at fault or the window was devoid of the attachment. Turning, he surveyed the chamber. It was small, fitted with the minimum of furniture, a place with a window, a door, a bed and little else. The Toymaster was either expressing his indifference or knew more about the Cyclan than he admitted. Luxury was something any cyber could do without.

Creel touched the bracelet locked about his left wrist. Invisible forces flowed from the instrument to set up a field that ensured that no electronic device could be focused in his vicinity. Spying ears and eyes would remain deaf and blind if they tried to pry into his room. Lying supine on the bed he closed his eyes and concentrated on the Samatchazi formulae. His breathing grew slower, shallow, regular as that of a man asleep. He gradually lost the use of his senses; had he opened his eyes he would have been blind. He floated, detached, unaffected by external reality. Within the confines of his skull his brain became a thing of pure intellect, its reasoning awareness his only connection with normal life. Only then did the grafted Homochon elements become active.

Creel entered a new sphere of existence. No two cybers had the same experience. It was something uniquely individual, impossible to either explain or fully communicate. For him it was as if he were a droplet in a universal sea, a mote drifting in a pulsing ocean of shimmering brilliance, each droplet shining with the pure light of intelligence. They swirled and rotated about a common centre, an inexhaustible sea reaching to infinity, and he was a part of it while it was a part of himself. He saw it, shared in it, belonged to it as one of a tremendous gestalt of living minds.

The centre was the pulsing heart of the Cyclan. Deeply buried in the heart of a lonely world, the central intelligence was the nexus from which streamed the complex power of the organisation of which it was the heart and brain. It touched his mental emissions, absorbed his knowledge as if he had been a squeezed sponge, took it, assimilated and correlated the data in a flickering instant of time. There was no verbal communication. Words were unnecessary, too slow, too tedious. Instead there was an instantaneous cerebral transmission against which the speed of light was a veritable crawl.

Financial pressure unnecessary at this time. Events moving to culmination of desired aim. Use to full advantage.

A question.

Use any and all means to achieve desired end. Failure will not be tolerated.

That was all.

The rest was an ecstasy of mental intoxication.

After rapport, during the time when the Homochon elements sank back into quiescence and the machinery of the body began to reassociate itself with mental control, there always came this period of supreme enlightenment. Creel floated in a darkening nothingness while he sensed strange memories and unlived situations, caught flashes of eerie thought concepts. Scraps of overflow from other minds, the residue of powerful intelligences, were caught and transmitted by the power of central intelligence, the tremendous cybernetic a complex that was the power of the Cyclan.

One day he would be a part of that nexus.

Creel opened his eyes and looked at the ceiling, seeing not the carved surface but his own future. His body would age and die, but his brain would be salvaged, incorporated in central intelligence, there to remain living and aware, a unit among countless other such units. A part of a superior brain, sharing and belonging to each and every other living mind in the entire network of freed intelligences

His reward. The reward of every cyber — if they did not fail.

5

There were guards at the gate, a small knot of men talking, lounging at their ease. Dumarest looked at them, at the ships resting on the landing field beyond, graceful silhouettes against the lightening sky. The guards were no real problem; there were other ways to get on the field and once among the ships he could contact a handler, arrange for a Low passage. But he could do nothing without money.

He looked around. A short distance from the gate the monks of the Universal Brotherhood had set up their portable church on a patch of cleared ground. Half a dozen men stood in line outside, waiting to enter, to sit beneath the benediction light, to confess their sins. Hypnotised, they would suffer subjective penance, gain comfort and mental ease, receive the traditional bread of forgiveness. Most of them, Dumarest knew, were more interested in getting the wafer of nutritious concentrate than easing their souls, but to get it they had to accept the hypnotic conditioning against violence to their fellows. The monks considered it a fair exchange.

He fell into line, hearing the low murmur of voices coming from the interior of the church. The man ahead, thin, pale, bearing the obvious marks of malnutrition, turned as Dumarest nudged him in the back

'Take it easy, mister. You're not the only one who's hungry.'

'I want information,' said Dumarest. 'Have any ships left since yesterday afternoon?'

'Maybe. What's the information worth?'

'A broken arm if you don't give it,' said Dumarest curtly. He'd walked five miles in biting cold since leaving the raft and his temper was getting short. 'And tell me the truth,' he added. 'I'll know if you lie.'

The man hesitated, saw the pale, strained face, the scarred clothing. 'All right,' he said. 'You don't have to get tough about it. One ship left yesterday. A small freighter bound for Toris.'

'All right. Now where can I find Mother Jocelyn?'

A dirty thumb jerked over a shoulder. 'Her place is down there. The house with a turret. But unless you've got money you'll be wasting your time.'

Early as it was the establishment was open for business. It was, Dumarest guessed, never closed. A place mainly catering to those who rode Middle, the men who crewed the metal eggs which travelled the gulfs between the stars; a taste of adventure for those who spent their lives in a grey monotony of emptiness.

He pushed open the door, stepped into a vestibule warm with circulated heat. Soft music drifted through the air, the wail of pipes, the beat of drums, the metallic clashing of cymbals. The air held a jungle-scent, raw, lush, animal. Womb-shaped, the vestibule reached from the door to a wide desk.

'Your pleasure, master?' The reception-ist was young, superbly shaped, black rippling hair framing an olive face. 'We have analogues to suit all requirements. Pain, fear, torture, death. We can give you the sensory excitement of a harem, a battle, invigorating delights of a hundred kinds.' Her voice chilled as Dumarest came closer. 'What do you want?'

'Mother Jocelyn.'

'You have an appointment?'

Dumarest leaned forward, his hands resting lightly on the desk. 'Don't play with me, girl. Just tell your boss that I want to see her.'

She swallowed. 'Your business?'

'Private.' Dumarest straightened, turned as a man entered the vestibule from a side door. He wore the uniform of an engineer. His eyes were glazed, unfocussed. He walked unsteadily, as if he was not quite sober.

'Wonderful,' he said, looking at Dumarest 'I've never known anything like it. Take my advice and try number thirty-one. Expensive but it's worth it. Number thirty-one.' He weaved past on his way to the door.

Dumarest turned back to the girl. Her eyes met his own, as level as the laser she held in her hand. 'You will take three steps backward,' she said. 'Away from the desk. If you do not move I shall burn you between the eyes. I am a very good shot,' she added. 'At this range it would be impossible for me to miss. Now move!'

He relaxed his knees, dropped and fell forward across the desk, snatched the weapon from her all in one swift movement.

She looked at him with incredulous eyes. 'Fast,' she said. 'I have never seen anyone as fast.'

'Nor as desperate,' he said grimly. He rested the laser on the edge of the desk. 'Now may I see your boss?'

* * *

Mother Jocelyn sat primly upright in her chair. She weighed no more than a child, skin tight over the bones of her face, eyes deeply set in their sockets. A crimped wig sat on her skull. Her hands were thin, heavily veined, glittering with rings. A voluminous dress of purple and gold masked her figure. She looked at Dumarest as he was ushered into her room.

'Your business must be very urgent for you to have taken such risks,' she said. Her voice was a piping treble. 'I hope for your sake that you are not wasting your time.'

'The importance is relative, my lady.' Dumarest glanced at the guards standing to either side. 'We have a mutual friend,' he said abruptly. 'A man named Legrain.'

'Mac Legrain?'

'That is the one. I want to find him.'

'You owe him something?' The thin voice held amusement. 'It must be a heavy debt for you to have taken so much trouble. You realise that you could have been killed downstairs? That you could still be killed?' Abruptly she gestured to the guards. 'You may leave us,' and then, to Dumarest, 'Mac Legrain is a friend of mine. You believe that?'

Dumarest shook his head. 'No, my lady. What would a person such as yourself have in common with a man like Legrain? You may be business associates, nothing more.'

'Not even that,' she admitted. 'He has been a customer here and that is all. If he told you otherwise he lied.' She dropped her hand to a carved box resting on a small table at her side, lifted the lid, took out a slender tube that she placed between her lips. A thin, acrid scent filled the air. 'Malash,' she said. 'You know of it?'

'Yes, my lady.'

'In time it will kill me,' she said. 'But beneath its influence, I am young again.' Sucking thoughtfully she stared at Dumarest. 'Yesterday,' she mused. 'About this time or maybe a little later. Two men managed to escape from the arena. They killed three men doing it and put another in the hospital.'

Dumarest made no comment.

'The guards are searching the city,' she said casually. 'Do you know what happens to men who do a thing like that?'

'You are going to tell me,' said Dumarest.

'They get thrown into the pens. Food for the weavers.' Her eyes were bright as they watched him over her tube. 'Spiders,' she explained. 'Ugly brutes as large as your head and with an appetite for living flesh. It is not an easy death. I have,' she added, 'an analogue of the experience for those with masochistic tendencies. Number eighteen. It is not in great demand.'

'No,' said Dumarest dryly. 'I can understand why not.'

'The best thing those men could do would be to leave Toy as quickly as possible.' She lifted a ringed hand, removed the tube from her lips, studied its tip. It was charred with chemical heat, the inhaled oxygen breaking the narcotic compound into its active constituents. 'It could be arranged,' she said softly. 'It would depend on many factors but it could be arranged.'

'Tell me where I can find Legrain and you'll have the money,' promised Dumarest.

'Money?' Gently she shook her head. 'Did I mention money? There are other forms of payment, my friend. You are strong, fast, ruthless. Only such a man could have escaped the arena. A good subject for an analogue. The battle,' she said. 'You must have fought well. And perhaps there are other adventures you have experienced which could be of value. A trade,' she suggested. 'A passage for an analogue. A fair exchange.'

Dumarest hesitated. Analogues were usually taken at the time of the experience, machines recording mental and physical detail. Such a recording could be played back to a receptive mind, the recipient seeming to actually live the recorded experience. Surrogate adventure, better than real life because predictable and safe. Death, even, vicariously enjoyed.

'You hesitate,' she said sharply. 'You are afraid? No,' she amended, looking at him. 'Not afraid. Cautious. You do not trust me?'

'My lady,' he said frankly, 'life has given me little cause to trust anyone.'

'You are wise,' she said, unruffled. 'There is no honour among thieves — as you have reason to know.' She replaced the tube between her lips, sucking hard so as to fill her lungs with the euphoric vapour. 'A pity,' she commented. 'An hour with my technicians and your troubles would be over.'

And that, he thought grimly, *is exactly what I'm afraid of. She wants to read my mind, snatch what is useful and leave what is not. But how careful would she be? What damage would she cause? What interest could she have in keeping me sane and well? No,* he decided. *There has to be another way to get off Toy.*

The same guards who had ushered him into the woman's presence ushered him out, leading him down corridors lined with doors which leaked disturbing noises: groans, screams, laughter, a soft whimpering, other, less human sounds. Customers locked in their worlds of make-believe, paying to enjoy or suffer another's pleasure or pain. Emotional ghouls.

The receptionist looked up as he entered the vestibule, her eyes cold, distant. He walked down the womb-like room, to the door, the cold air of the street.

Into the arms of the waiting guards.

★ ★ ★

Restern's face was taut on the screen. 'Leon. Have you heard the news?' His lack of the usual punctilious address betrayed his agitation. Leon leaned back in his chair and looked at his caller. 'No,' he said. 'I haven't heard anything of interest. I've been at the factory all morning,' he explained. 'Since shortly after dawn. What is it?'

'Mulwo's dead. Sheem called and discovered the body.'

Leon frowned. 'How do you mean? Where was he? Where were his servants?'

'Gone,' said Restern curtly. 'His personal valet was found in the bath with his throat cut. His bed-slave had been shot with a laser. The rest had vanished. We'll find them,' he said after a pause. 'But it's obvious what the story will be. The valet went insane, perhaps through jealousy. He shot the girl and Mulwo, then killed himself.'

'After terrifying the others to make them run.' Leon frowned, thoughtful. 'How many were there? Mulwo didn't maintain a large town establishment, as I remember.'

'Not since his wife died. His only son is out at the estate. Sheem is calling to break the news. My guess is that there'd be only four or five more servants. Six at the most. His raft is missing,' he added. 'The pilot also.'

'Naturally,' said Leon dryly. 'The one who did this had no desire to leave witnesses.'

'You don't think it was as it appears?'

'Do you?' Leon met Restern's eyes. 'Who is working on the case? Commander Gyrn of the city guards?'

Restern nodded.

'Then we know what the verdict is going to be. The missing servants will never be found. Mulwo was killed by his valet, who then cut his throat, probably forgetting he held a laser. Before doing that he somehow managed to terrify all the rest of the servants into getting aboard the raft; they headed out to sea and there drowned themselves.' His fist made a drumming sound as he slammed it on the desk. 'Raw,' he said. 'Too raw. Does he think we are all fools?'

'Groshen?'

'Who else?' Leon sat, drumming his fingers, wondering how much to tell the other man. Nothing at all, he decided. With an obvious traitor in the cabal no precaution could be too stringent. But to him it was obvious what had happened and why it had been done. A warning, he thought grimly. The one who had advocated armed rebellion was dead. Who would be next?

'Listen,' he said to the anxious face on the screen. 'There is nothing we can do, therefore we shall do nothing. Aside from sending the usual condolences, of course. Do you know how his son wishes to dispose of the body? Cremation? Converting it into a Figure? Of course, you couldn't know that yet,' he said, remembering. 'The Association must send a tribute.' He shook his head. 'This is bad,' he said. 'Mulwo was a good man.'

Restern cleared his throat. 'Perhaps,' he said carefully, 'we shouldn't make too much of that.'

'No.' Leon was emphatic. 'He worked with us,' he explained. 'We saw much of each other. He was a personal friend to you, me, others. To deny that now would be to admit we knew him to be an enemy of the Toymaster.' He paused. 'To do that,' he said softly, 'will be to act like

115

dogs on the run. I, Stockholder Restern, am not a dog.'

'My apologies if any words of mine could have inferred that you are, Stockholder Hurl.'

'I accept your apology.' Ritual, thought Leon. But it had its uses. It kept men facing reality if nothing else. But I shouldn't blame him too much, he thought. I had the benefit of advance knowledge. This does not come as the surprise it does to him. Him and the others, he thought. The next meeting of the cabal could well be its last. Frightened men made poor conspirators and Mulwo's death would give them cause for fear. Unless . . . ?

'I have some business to conduct,' he said. 'I may need to contact you in haste. You will be at home?'

Restern shook his head. 'No,' he said. 'Your advice is good. I shall be working as usual. That,' he added grimly, 'or I shall be under interrogation.'

It was a likely probability. The Toymaster was not the sort of man to ease up once he had someone on the run, Leon reflected as he hung up.

A call brought his raft to the door. He climbed in, settled back on the cushions, snapped an order to the pilot. 'The Library.'

'At once, Stockholder.'

Leon relaxed as the raft hummed high into the sky. To one side he could see the city, wide streets and beautiful buildings, spacious and gracious, a machine designed for luxurious living, the landing field and warehouses discreetly placed to one extremity. Or at least, he reminded himself, that was how it had been in the beginning. Now hovels rested where open spaces had looked at the sky. Ugliness and squalor had shamed the original conception.

And it had been a wonderful conception. True, the Director of Grail had given his son the world as a plaything, but the boy had had a love of beauty and he had been guided by older minds. Guided but not trammelled. He had done his best to build a utopia.

He had almost succeeded, thought Leon. Had succeeded for the first few generations before the race had become contaminated and the population divided into those who held stock and those who did not. Broodingly Leon thought of the Figures at home in his country palace: the bodies of his ancestors, treated so as to render them proof against corruption, which sat at the long table in the Hall of Memories. They had known the good times of building, the exciting times of vigorous growth. They had died peacefully of age, honourably in combat, but how many had felt the vile touch of an assassin?

What would they have thought of the lunatic progress of the present Toymaster?

'The Library, Stockholder.' The voice of the pilot broke into his retrospection. He guided the raft into a wide lazy circle. 'The main entrance, Stockholder?'

'No.' That would be too crowded, thronged with those who wished to hire the services of the machine, busy with agents acting on the behalf of clients light-years away. 'The technicians' entrance,' he decided. And if Vohmis didn't like it that was just too bad.

There were the usual formalities. Leon stood, controlling his impatience as a technician checked his identity against the master role. Like a priest, he thought. A guardian of one of the old religions. A temple keeper jealous of his prerogatives, automatically against anyone who did not belong to the cult of which he was a member. And the Librarians were a cult, a closed circle of those who could operate and maintain the machine. *You can't blame them*. Leon told himself. *They are working for the common good, for all the residents of Toy.*

And yet he was irritated. He was a stockholder with all its attendant privileges. He had the right of access to the Library at any time.

'Stockholder Hurl!' Vohmis, the Head Librarian, rose as Leon entered his office. He was old, skin dulled with the passage of years spent poring over his charts and graphs in his sunless office. *A human mole*, thought Leon. *A man who never left the precincts of the Library*. 'This is an unusual pleasure.'

'One that has been delayed too long, Stockholder Vohmis,' responded Leon politely. 'I must thank you for your prediction in regard to my patterns. The melange is an unusual bloom.' He hesitated, then: 'One that is of limited popularity. I trust there can be no mistake?'

'None!' Vohmis was always quick to defend his predictions. Too quick, thought Leon. He pressed a little harder.

'Odd that the prediction should have changed so abruptly. You are certain as to the validity of the new data? I ask,' he said, 'because of the importance of the change. We do not want to be loaded with unsaleable designs.'

'The prediction is accurate,' said Vohmis. He returned to his desk, sat, toyed with the sheaves of paper which always cluttered the flat surface. 'You need have no fears on that score, Stockholder Hurl.'

'My apologies if I unwittingly questioned your integrity,' said Leon. 'I accept your apology.'

'You have a position of tremendous responsibility,' said Leon, sitting without waiting for an invitation. 'In a sense you are the real ruler of Toy. The financial ruler,' he hastened to add. 'A wrong prediction and the dividend would suffer. Too many of them and our wealth would dissipate. And it would take so little,' he mused. 'A scrap of faulty data. A misleading fact. Information that turned out to be inaccurate. Information,' he said meaningfully, 'which could originate from someone who has not the welfare of Toy at heart.'

'You are talking of the changed prediction,' said Vohmis shrewdly. 'The data came direct from the Toymaster.'

'From Groshen?' Leon leaned forward in his chair. 'Or,' he said softly, 'from the cyber Creel?'

Vohmis hesitated. 'From the cyber,' he admitted 'But I checked,' he hastened to add. 'By ultra-wave with Artus. What the cyber said is true.'

'Of course.' Leon backed, smiling, casually. 'What else could it be? A lie at this time would defeat his purpose. It would rob him of the regard of the Toymaster. No, Stockholder Vohmis. The cyber will not lie, not yet.'

Vohmis snatched at the bait. 'You think he will later?'

'I mention it as a possibility,' said Leon smoothly. 'On an assumption based, I will admit, on suspicion rather than fact. But if the Toymaster should come to rely on the cyber, choose his predictions over your own, what then? The Library will not be as it is now.' He laughed, shrugging. 'But who knows what the cyber will do? Or the Toymaster?'

'It might,' said Vohmis slowly, 'be possible to find out.'

'An analogue, you mean?' Leon looked thoughtful. 'I hadn't considered that,' he lied. 'But now that you mention it I assume it would not be hard for you to run a few problems through the machine based on assumed data. What would happen if the cyber should lie in some probable future, for example.' He shook his head, gesturing with his hands. 'But I hardly need to tell you what to do. You, better than any man on Toy, need no such advice.'

Flattery, he thought. The cheapest coin

of intrigue but still the most reliable. Appeal to a man's ego. Hold up a mirror so that he can see his image in gross exaggeration. Plant a seed of doubt, of suspicion and let it grow as grow it must. Point out that the cyber was the Librarian's greatest enemy, hint as to why, leave the rest to the highly developed survival instinct of the stockholders of Toy.

But now it was time to change the subject. He leaned forward, looking with interest at a small model half hidden by the papers on the desk. 'Something new, Stockholder Vohmis?'

'This?' The Librarian picked it up, turned it in his hands. Made of transparent plastic, it held odd, distorted lines. Leon tried to follow what appeared to be a convoluted tube, lost it, blinked suddenly aching eyes. 'An experiment in three-dimensional topography,' said Vohmis. 'An idea of the Toymaster's. We are building it close to the machine.'

Leon frowned.

'It was Groshen's direct order,' said Vohmis. 'He said that the tunnels would be of later use for the storage of needed memory banks. He has a point,' he admitted, setting down the model. 'Excavations are costly and we always seek extra capacity.'

'But what is it?'

'A maze.' Vohmis gently touched the model. 'An interesting development utilising the principles of both the moebius strip and the Klein bottle. Two and three-dimensional objects which have only one surface,' he explained. 'I am surprised that you did not know about it.'

'The Toymaster rarely takes me into his confidence,' said Leon dryly. 'On such a matter as this I would have been compelled to object on the basis of its close proximity to the machine. As you should have done,' he pointed out.

Vohmis took offence. 'Are you imputing that I lack courage?'

'No,' said Leon quickly. 'I apologise for any implication my words may have contained.'

'I accept your apology.' Vohmis shook off the stiffness of formality. 'I did protest,' he admitted. 'But the Toymaster insisted, claiming that the area could be put to later use. Also, as it is being built by my technicians, it would have been inconvenient at any great distance.'

'A maze,' said Leon thoughtfully. 'A toy. But what is its purpose?'

'Does a plaything need a purpose?' Vohmis was cynical.

'No,' admitted Leon, 'But normally it has one.' He frowned, thinking. Utilising laser-power excavations took little time and specialised machines spraying plastic soon sealed the raw tunnels. More tedious was the installation of air-conditioning and other facilities. 'How far has it progressed?' he asked casually.

Vohmis shrugged. 'It is almost finished. A few days and it will be complete.'

'When was it begun?'

'Before Creel arrived on Toy,' said Vohmis shrewdly, guessing what was in Leon's mind. 'The cyber had no hand in this.'

'Then who did?' Leon touched the model with the tip of his finger. 'Groshen is no scientist. He could never have designed this himself. Someone must have given him the idea.'

'A traveller, perhaps?' Vohmis shrugged; to him the question was of no importance. 'A seller of novelties or a topologist who managed to catch the Toymaster's attention. But the thing is clever,' he said reluctantly. 'An incredible amount of surface area compressed into a small volume of space.' He pushed aside the model, looked at his visitor. 'You will forgive me, Stockholder Hurl, but there are matters which require my attention.'

Leon smiled, recognising the ritual formula for parting, but he wasn't going to let Vohmis escape him so soon.

'There is another matter,' he said casually. 'I wish to consult the Library.'

'A personal consultation?' The Librarian made an effort to mask his annoyance. 'Every outlet is fully booked, Stockholder Hurl. It would be most inconvenient to alter the schedules. If it is a matter which could wait I will personally attend to it as soon as possible.'

Leon was curt. 'This matter permits of no delay.'

'But . . . ?'

'I apologise for any offence,' interrupted Leon, 'but much as I hate to inconvenience you, I must insist on my right as a stockholder of Toy to consult the Library as and when I wish.'

Vohmis bowed, accepting defeat. 'As you wish, Stockholder Hurl. What do you wish to ask?'

'Several questions,' said Leon blandly. 'One of them being the predicted time of my death.'

6

A man lay whimpering, crying, the tears streaming down his face. 'No,' he pleaded. 'Oh, no. Please no.'

He was ignored by the four men playing cards, the two playing chess. A thickset, burly man dressed in stained leather clothing looked over at Dumarest.

'Crazy,' he explained. 'Used a chemical analogue and butchered his wife and kids. Now he's just beginning to realise what he's done.' He turned at the sound of footsteps. 'Food,' he said. 'And about time too.'

It was stew, thick and nourishing if not fancy. Dumarest sat at the table with the others, eating from a soft plastic plate with a similar spoon. The cell was twenty feet square, lined on two sides with a dozen bunks, fitted with toilet facilities and washbasins. The air was warm, scented with the faintly acrid tang of disinfectants. Everything was spotlessly clean.

He had been in a lot worse places, decided Dumarest. He finished his stew, ate a second helping and pushed plate and spoon aside. Since his arrest he had eaten and slept. Now he wondered how long he would be kept waiting. Not long, he guessed; the appointments of the cell showed it to be a place for transients. To spend time in such a place would be no punishment.

A guard halted at the bars. 'Dumarest!'

'Here.'

'You're wanted. Step outside.' The guard stepped back as the door slid aside, closed again as Dumarest passed through into the corridor. Both ends were fitted with heavy bars behind which sat armed guards. There were no windows. Escape from the underground cellblock looked impossible. Dumarest's eyes were watchful as he followed the guard through barred gates and down narrow passages.

'Here.' The man halted, gestured at a door. 'Inside. Your advocate is waiting.'

He was small, delicate, his olive face as smooth as a woman's, his hands those of a child. He wore a colourful weave, and a pomander dangling from his left wrist. He held it beneath flaring nostrils, sniffing, his muddy brown eyes examining his client. A limp hand gestured to a chain. 'Be seated. I do not like a man to loom above me.'

Dumarest sat down.

'My name is Krailton,' said the dandy. 'I am to defend you at your trial.'

'I must tell you,' said Dumarest. 'I have no money to pay your fee.'

'I am aware of that. The matter has been attended to.'

'By whom?'

'There is an old proverb,' said Krailton blandly. 'One should never examine a gift beneath a microscope.'

Perhaps not, thought Dumarest, but some gifts cost too high a price. He frowned, thinking, Mother Jocelyn? Hardly. She must have sent for the guards even before she'd made her offer. They had waited discreetly outside like trained dogs ready to pounce. Stockholder Ledra? Why should she want to help him? But who else could it be?

'I cannot tell you,' said Krailton impatiently when Dumarest asked. 'The matter is confidential. I suggest that we concentrate on more important matters now. What is the nature of your defence? Not that you have any,' he said without waiting for an answer, 'but I am hopeful that something can be done. Are you accustomed to lying?'

'If the necessity arises,' said Dumarest curtly, 'I can lie.'

'Don't. The monitor will be able to gauge the veracity of your replies,' explained Krailton. 'There are electronic devices fitted to the dock. Justice on Toy is simple, fast and efficient. A criminal will condemn himself. If you cannot tell the truth say nothing at all. In fact,' he added, 'I insist on it. Silence, I mean. As your advocate I shall plead for you. Speak only if the monitor demands a direct answer. Do you understand?'

Dumarest nodded.

'I shall not delude you,' said the advocate. 'There is little hope. However, Monitor Thyle is not favourably disposed to the arena. It may be possible to save you from the pens.' He crossed to the door, opened it, stood looking at

Dumarest. 'Well,' he snapped impatiently. 'What are you waiting for'

Light streamed through the transparent roof of the courtroom. Dumarest squinted, stumbled as a guard led him toward a raised platform that was railed and ringed with vicious spikes. A throng of sightseers faced the bench where the monitor sat. The preliminaries were brief

'For the prosecution,' said a man dressed in shimmering black. 'The prisoner, being a member of the losing side in a battle conducted in the arena, did kill three men and injure a fourth, all innocent spectators and all unconnected with the battle in any way. He did then steal a raft . . . '

Dumarest looked around, not concentrating on the droned words of the arraignment. Legalistic procedure was much the same on all civilised worlds in that it followed the pattern of accusation and defence. He turned his attention to Krailton as the advocate climbed to his feet. Against the black of the court officials he was a blaze of defiant colour

'The arena,' he said, 'is an area divorced of all law but the law of survival, as this court and all men know. It follows that the so-called 'innocent men', those killed and injured by my client, by venturing into the precincts of the arena voluntarily surrendered the protection of Original Law. More, they, by adopting the role of hunters, reduced the status of the prisoner to that of an animal. An animal cannot be blamed for its nature. The men knew the risks inherent in what they did and tried to minimise it by the use of a raft and powerful weapons. They were careless. They fell to the nature of the beast. We submit there is no case to answer.'

Clever, thought Dumarest. His unknown benefactor had picked a good man. If the court accepted the basic premise he had put up a perfect defence.

The monitor cleared his throat. 'The court accepts the submission as to the charges of murder and mayhem. They will be stricken from the arraignment. However, there remains the matter of the raft.'

'Which we do not contest,' said Krailton quickly. 'It is true that the prisoner did steal the raft. However, in mitigation, I again plead the nature of the beast. To escape from imminent death is a matter of survival. To use any means to ensure that end must be accepted as a matter of principle.'

The prosecutor rose, sombre in his black, eyes gleaming with triumph. 'The pilot could, had he been requested, have flown the prisoner from the arena. Had escape been of prime importance and the sole motivation that is what would have happened. But the raft was stolen and has not been recovered. Who else but the prisoner was responsible for its loss? I contend that the charge of theft must remain.'

The monitor looked at Krailton, raised his eyebrows, glanced at the prosecutor. 'Is there anything else?'

'A complaint from Stockholder Ledra. The prisoner was given medical aid at her factory. Guessing the man was a criminal, she notified the authorities, arranging to hold him through the night for collection at dawn. Before then he escaped, doing certain damage and stealing another raft.'

'Which has been recovered,' said Krailton.

'Which has been recovered,' agreed the prosecutor. 'But the matter of damages remains to be assessed.'

The monitor leaned back in his chair, eyes raised to the ceiling, fingers toying with a stylo. 'Has the prisoner money?' he demanded.

Krailton stepped closer to the bench. 'None.'

'Then the matter of assessment of damages is academic. Yet the robbed man must be recompensed and so must the state.' He picked up a gavel. 'Therefore, by the regulations as laid down in Original Law, the prisoner is sentenced to be sold on the block at the next auction.' The gavel slammed down. 'Next case!'

★   ★   ★

Brother Elas stepped close to the cell and looked through the bars. 'Brother,' he said, 'you seem to be in a parlous state. Is there anything you need?'

'A gun,' said Dumarest. 'A means of

escape. A passage away from Toy.'

'Those things are beyond our power to provide, brother,' said the monk. 'Do you need medical aid? Counsel? A message carried to a friend?'

Dumarest shook his head. The man meant well but what could he do? Irritably he paced the narrow confines facing the bars. They hadn't taken him back to the spacious cell below after sentence now he was caged like an animal in a place only large enough for one. Other cells ran to either side. Strangers came and peered through the bars, assessing the value of the goods to be offered for sale. Among them, drab in their homespun robes, the monks moved quietly, offering what help they could.

'Are you of the church, brother?' Elas caught his eye gestured for him to come close.

'I don't make a habit of sitting beneath your benediction light,' said Dumarest shortly.

'And yet you are not unknown to us,' said the monk evenly. 'Do you believe in the virtue of forgiveness?'

'Of course.'

'There is one who seeks it, brother. From you. You will see him? Speak to him? He asked me to approach you, brother. He fears lest you betray him.' The monk turned, gestured. Legrain stepped into view.

He was smooth, sleek, neat in his new clothing of chocolate brown. Dumarest looked at him, knuckles white as he gripped the bars. Deliberately he relaxed. 'You,' he said flatly. 'This is a surprise.'

'I know how you feel, Earl.' Legrain stepped closer, his voice low. 'I took too long getting back to the cave. But you should have waited. My message told you to wait.'

'I saw no message.'

'But I left one. A scrap of fabric weighted with a stone. I pricked my finger to get something to write with.' Legrain held out his left hand. 'See? The wound is still open.'

Dumarest dropped his eyes, looked at the tiny cut. His hands fell from the bars. 'The wind must have blown it away,' he said. 'That or a bird must have taken it.

137

What happened?'

'You were sleeping,' said Legrain softly. 'Dead to the world. I figured that it would be best for me to sell the stuff as quickly as possible. Before the descriptions had been passed around. I wrote the message and flew to a place I know. The man I had to see was out. I waited, finally closed the deal and returned to the cave. You were gone. Honestly, Earl, I didn't know what to think. At first I wondered if they'd caught you. Then I thought that maybe you'd fallen into the sea.'

'And?'

'I was desperate. I knew that if you were still alive you'd head for the landing field so I had a couple of friends of mine keep watch. They saw you grabbed. I couldn't do anything but hire the advocate. He came expensive too,' he added. Took most of what I made on the deal. But it was the only way to save you from the pens.'

'And half of it was mine anyway, of course,' reminded Dumarest. He frowned. 'How did you expect to get me out of the cave if you'd sold the raft?'

'I'd hired another. That was part of the deal. I intended to throw down a rope from the top of the cliff. But I left it too late. I'm sorry, Earl,' he said. 'All I can say is that I did my best.'

'I suppose I should thank you,' said Dumarest slowly. 'You'll understand why I don't feel grateful.'

'You saved my life,' said Legrain. 'But for you I'd be lying dead in the arena. If you'd talked I'd be with you in that cell. Don't you think I feel bad at what's happened? Listen,' he said. 'I could have shipped out. A freighter headed for Toris. I could have been on it. But I stayed, hung around in case I could be of use.' His hand came through the bars, open, inviting. 'All right, Earl?'

Dumarest gripped the hand, squeezed. 'All right,' he said. 'What happens now?'

'You get sold,' said Legrain. 'Put up on the block, knocked down to the highest bidder. The state takes its cut and passes over the rest to those who have a claim against you for damages. If the sum obtained is higher than what you owe the balance is put to your credit. It's the way they settle debts here,' he explained. 'If a man owes what he can't pay then he's sold. Women too. Some of them get a better deal out of being a slave than they could ever hope to get by remaining free. And you can always buy yourself out of bondage. Your owner has to release you as soon as you give him your purchase price. That's the law.'

Dumarest looked at the monk. 'Could you do that? Pay what I owe? I swear that you will get back whatever it costs.'

Regretfully Brother Elas shook his head. 'Earlier, brother, it could have been done. Stockholder Hurl was most generous in giving us the balance of his dividend. But we bought food, medicines, clothing, a host of immediate necessities.'

It was normal procedure, thought Dumarest. The Universal Brotherhood did not hoard wealth.

★   ★   ★

Sunlight, blazing, splintering from the stone of the square, shimmering from the brilliant weaves worn by those thronging the

140

area, reflected in a thousand shades of kaleidoscopic colour from the glassite walls, the windows, the tinkling fountains. Naked, Dumarest looked down from his raised platform. He stood in line with a dozen others from the prison, each chained to the other by a thin manacle. Bodies white and olive, brown and ebony black, all waiting to be sold.

'A farmer,' said the auctioneer. He was a tall, thin, elderly man wearing spotless white, a man fully conscious of the dignity of his position. 'A man of youth yet experienced in the growing of crops and the tilling of the soil. Gentles, I await your offers.'

A hand rose, another, several in quick succession as voices stated the price they were willing to pay for the young man.

'A bad time for auction, this,' said the man standing behind Dumarest. 'The dividend is almost due. That means they've the rest of their credit to get rid of. Price now has no meaning.'

And the higher the price the greater the difficulty of getting free, thought Dumarest. If a slave could ever hope to earn a respectable sum at all. No owner would be stupid enough to lose a good investment — and a slave could not demand payment for services rendered.

'An engineer,' said the auctioneer, his voice carried by electronic apparatus hidden in his rostrum. 'Old but with many years of skill living in his fingers and many years of service yet to give. Gentles, this man would grace any factory. Your offers, if you please.'

Hands lifted among the gaily dressed throng. Laughter echoed above the tinkling of the fountains. Holidaymakers, thought Dumarest. Men and women out for a little fun, degenerates looking for fleshy targets, the bored for something to ease their boredom. To them the prisoners were animals, some amusing, some beautiful, none to be considered as wholly human.

Dumarest restrained his anger. Rage was a luxury no slave could afford.

The chain jerked his wrist. He mounted the steps to the higher rostrum, eyes searching the crowd as the old man droned his preliminary to asking for offers. He could see no recognisable face, but that meant nothing. Neither Stockholder Ledra or Mother Jocelyn need buy in person.

A man lifted his arm, called an offer. Immediately it was topped. A woman screamed her bid, swore at the ribald comments and bid again. The auctioneer sucked in his breath with satisfaction. Not often did he sell such a prize.

'A fighting man,' he said again. 'One who has both fought and escaped from the arena. Now, Gentles, let us not tarry.'

Again the woman bid, a man, another man, a young girl with a ravaged face, a crone ridiculous in her finery. Dumarest looked at none of them. A jerk at the chain told when the bidding was over.

'You did well,' said the guard as he slipped off the manacle. 'Full damages and something over. The cost of a Low passage at least.'

The cost of a passage, thought Dumarest grimly. Escape — but no chance of using it. He stared at his owner, a swarthy man with crimped and oiled hair, cicatrices on his face.

'I am Techon,' he said. 'A fair man. Work well, cause no trouble, and we shall get along fine.' He nodded to a servant. The slave was of the same breed as the Toymaster's guards, seven feet tall, superbly muscled but with a loose, vacuous expression. A halfwit, thought Dumarest. A reject. More an animal than a man. He stepped back as the slave reached for his throat.

'Steady,' warned Techon. 'Krul only wants to fit you with a collar. The same as he wears, see?' He lifted the cane he carried and touched the metal band around the slave's neck. 'You can let him fit it,' he said casually. 'Or he will knock you down and do it just the same. Is a broken jaw worth a moment of useless resistance?'

Dumarest remained silent, letting the slave fit the collar, feeling the smooth, flexible metal clamp snugly around his throat.

'You are a man of sense,' said Techon. 'Now slip on this robe. If these sex-hungry bitches want to see a real man they'll have to pay for the privilege.' He nodded as Dumarest fastened the thin, knee-length robe of cheap fibre. 'You're thin,' he said. 'Wasted. But we'll soon fix that. Now follow me.'

A raft stood waiting outside the area. It lifted them, dropped them on the flat roof of a low building. Inside was an odd mixture of spartan simplicity and extravagant luxury. Small bedrooms held a narrow cot and little else while others, ten times the size, were draped in blazing weave, the wide beds a mass of feathery cushions, the appointments to match.

'For visitors,' explained Techon. He slammed the door and led the way down a passage. 'They come here to be entertained. It is strange the fascination an athlete can hold for a certain type of person. But I cater to them as a sideline. My profession is that of fightmaster.'

He led the way to the ground level. A padded door gave onto a small room smelling faintly of sweat and oil. Beyond it lay another, much larger, fitted with hanging ropes, mats, apparatus designed to strengthen muscle.

'This,' said Techon, 'is where you will

train.' Abruptly, without warning, he slashed viciously at Dumarest's face with his cane. It whistled unimpeded through the air as he ducked. 'Good,' said the fightmaster. 'You are fast. Or perhaps it was luck. We shall see. Krul!'

The slave trotted to the side of the room, returned bearing rods, two thin ones of metal and one of much thicker wood. He handed the wooden one to Dumarest.

'This is what we shall do,' said Techon. 'Krul and I will try to hit you with these steel rods. You will do your best to defend yourself against them with the one of wood. Ready?'

'A moment.' Dumarest rested the tip of his rod on the floor, stamped down with his bare foot. The rod snapped halfway down its length. Throwing aside one piece he poised the other.

Techon narrowed his eyes. 'You are accustomed to the knife?'

'I have had cause to use one a few times.'

'And so consider yourself an expert, no doubt.' The fightmaster sucked in his lips.

'Well, we shall see.'

He sprang forward, slashed, thrust, slashed again, the steel rod whining through the air.

Dumarest protected himself with quick movements of the stick, the impact of metal on wood making a series of sharp, rapping sounds. He grunted as Krul joined in, the thin, whip-like rod burning across his shoulders. He backed in an effort to face both men, slowing, sweat glistening on his face as they speeded and coordinated their attack. Blood showed on the thin robe as lashing steel lacerated the skin beneath.

'You are not as good as you imagined, my friend,' commented Techon as his rod cracked home. 'Fast, yes, but not fast enough. And you are a little clumsy, but that could be because of lack of training.' He stepped back. 'Krul! Enough!'

The slave reluctantly discontinued his attack.

'Strip,' ordered the fightmaster to Dumarest.

He pursed his lips as he examined his new possession. On the white skin the weals stood out, dark with congested blood. 'A hundred hours of subjective treatment beneath slow time,' he decided. 'Three hours of normal. Expensive, but I think it's worth it in this case. In any event we have no time to lose. The Toymaster has demanded a spectacle for the entertainment of his guests and I am not a man to let him down.' His hand made a meaty sound as he slapped Dumarest on the shoulder. 'Treatment, then hard training. You agree?'

Dumarest was curt. 'Have I any choice?'

'No, but a willing fighter is a good fighter. I didn't pay what I did for a fool to be butchered to amuse the ladies There will be heavy wagers. I want to win a lot of money. We want to win a lot of money.' Again his hand slapped the shoulder. 'Cake for the master, crumbs for the slave, admitted, but that's life.' His eyes searched Dumarest's face. 'You object to being called a slave?'

'No. I object to being treated like one.'

'Proud,' commented Techon. 'Well, pride has its uses, but not in my establishment.' He rested the fingers of his right hand on the instrument strapped to his left. 'There is one lesson you have yet to learn,' he said softly. 'To obey. To go to your death if I order it. But to obey always.'

'And if I do not?'

'This,' said Techon.

Pain blazed from the collar around Dumarest's throat as the fightmaster adjusted the instrument. A red tide of screaming agony tore at every nerve and cell of his brain. Dumarest dropped to his knees, hands tearing vainly at the band around his throat.

'And this,' said the fightmaster softly.

Dumarest cried out as fresh agony rasped along nerve and sinew, doubling him in helpless writhing, filling the universe with an encompassing flood of unbearable torment.

7

Leon Hurl lifted the delicate porcelain of the cup and carefully savoured the steaming bouquet. *Odd* he thought. *I must have taken tea at least forty thousand times during my life, but how often have I really appreciated what I drank?*

He sniffed again, flaring his nostrils, brows creased as he tried to identify the spice. Some frenshi, perhaps? Certainly more than a little wenclin. A touch of gish and a suspicion of honeydew. He must remember to ask.

He sipped, letting the hot, spiced tea lave his palate before it slid down his throat to warm his stomach, then swallowed the rest and put down the empty cup. Rising, he walked around the room. He had deliberately arrived early so as to give himself time to think, but it wasn't wholly that. He wanted time to see something else. A desire to inspect the room in which he had so often sat. See it without the distraction of others, the cabal, the other members of the Spinners Association.

It seemed larger now that he was alone. He carefully examined the warmgrained wood, the intricacies of the carved ceiling, seeing in both something he had never noticed before: *Waste,* he thought. *Men spend their lives creating beauty for the enjoyment of others and we are all too busy to appreciate what they have done. What they have left us. Too eager for the future to spare any time for, the past.*

He turned, slowly, eyes drinking in what he saw. From now it would always be like this. He would taste everything he ate and swallowed, study everything he saw, weigh each word spoken and heard, each sound, each little modulation. For him every second had become a precious jewel to hold as long as he was able. And yet what had really changed?

Nothing but a temporal shift in an objective viewpoint. Simply that.

He turned as Evan came bursting into the room. 'Leon! Why did you call a special meeting? What is wrong?'

'Nothing is wrong,' said Leon quietly. He gestured to where the pot and cups stood on a small table against the wall. 'Will you join me in tea?'

Impatiently Mere Evan shook his head. 'There must be something wrong,' he insisted stubbornly. 'Why else would you call another meeting so soon after the last? What is it? Stockholder Hurl, I demand to know!'

'Demand?' Leon raised his eyebrows. 'Stockholder Evan, I take offence at your tone.'

'My apologies,' said Evan quickly. 'I am distraught. Mulwo's death you understand.' He trailed off, spread his hands. 'Please. If it is a matter of importance I should know. As a member of the Association I have a right to know.'

'And know you shall.' Leon crossed to the small table, poured himself more tea. How, he wondered, could he have tolerated the fool for so long? Tolerance, he thought. The secret of all successful civilisations. But could a plan for living be considered a success when it forced a man to quell his natural desires? His natural reactions?

Sheem, Amish, others of the group entered the room as he finished his tea. Soon all were gathered except Restern. Leon cleared his throat, called the meeting to order.

Evan objected. 'Stockholder Restern, our chairman, is not yet present.'

'Nor will he be,' said Sheem sombrely. 'At this moment he is being interrogated by Commander Gyrn of the city guard.' He glanced around the table. 'I have no objection to Stockholder Hurl's conducting this meeting. Has anyone else?' He waited, nodded to Leon. 'There are no objections, Stockholder Hurl. Please continue. We are in your hands.'

Not quite, thought Leon. *In someone's hands, yes, but we have yet to find out whose. Not that it matters*, he told himself. *Not now.*

'You must all have learned by now of Stockholder Mulwo's death,' he said without preamble. 'You may even have heard the official version of what is assumed to have happened. Some of you may believe it. I do not. I would be interested to know how many of you share my opinion that Stockholder Mulwo was assassinated by order of the Toymaster?'

He counted hands.

'Unanimous. Stockholder Restern is at this moment being interrogated. Could anyone suggest why?' He looked at Evan. 'You perhaps?'

Evan shook his head.

Sheem broke the silence. 'Stockholder Mulwo, in this very room, spoke of raising a group of mercenaries and instigating an armed rebellion. Stockholder Restern was the chairman at the time. The two incidents have an obvious connection.'

'Very obvious,' said Amish dryly. 'Stockholder Mulwo was killed because of his traitorous suggestion and Stockholder Restern is in trouble because he did not report what was said and therefore can be considered to have agreed with it.'

'Exactly.' Leon looked around the table. 'But who did report it?' he asked softly. 'Who, in this room, is a spy for the Toymaster?'

A man spoke from the far end of the table. 'Must it be one of us? Could not the room have been under surveillance?'

'No.' Sheem spoke without waiting for the chairman's permission. 'The room was electronically sealed. This I swear.'

'It could have been a servant,' suggested another. 'A man in the pay of Commander Gyrn. A woman even. Stockholder Mulwo was not in the habit of lowering his voice.'

'And neither are you,' snapped Amish. He had been a close friend of the dead man. 'If you take offence,' he added, 'I am ready and willing to meet any action you may contemplate.'

'Please!' Leon slammed his hand hard on the table, his voice rising above the hollow booming of the wood. 'We are not here to quarrel among ourselves. The situation is too serious for that. Stockholder Amish, you will apologise.'

Amish scowled, then shrugged. 'As you direct, Stockholder Hurl.' He turned to the man at his side. 'I apologise for any offence my words may have caused.'

'Your apology is accepted.'

Children, thought Leon. *But protocol is important to a child. Our ancestors knew their own nature when they devised the ritual. It places a barrier between thought and action, between word and deed. Hot tempers need a tight rein.*

'I did not summon you here to indulge in mutual recrimination,' he said coldly.

'There are facts we must face and decisions we must make.'

'The spy,' said Evan wildly. 'We must discover who is the spy!'

'What good will that do us now?' Leon shook his head. 'His reports have been made. We are all as guilty as Restern and the Toymaster knows as much as we do. Almost as much,' he corrected. 'There is one thing which his spy does not know. His treachery will not save him. He is already as good as dead.' He fell silent, waiting, continuing as no one spoke.

'We do not need to worry about the spy,' he said evenly. 'The Toymaster is not a man to nurture danger. A man who betrays once will do so again, and the hire of an assassin comes cheaper than the transfer of stock.' He searched faces with his eyes. Evan? Sheem? Amish? One of the others?

'I have consulted the Library,' he said abruptly. 'I asked certain questions. As you know, the machine can predict the future with an amazing degree of accuracy if given enough data. That is why I say we do not have to worry about the spy among us. I know his future as I know the future of us all.' He paused and again his eyes searched the watching faces.

'In one month from now,' he said deliberately; 'unless something untoward takes place, all of us now present in this room will be dead.'

★ ★ ★

Quara was waiting in the solar when he returned home. She rose from a chair, a kill-time toy spilling from her lap in a shower of brilliant sparkles. She was, he noted, wearing pearl and orange, the inevitable poniard at her belt. 'Leon!' Her eyes were penetrating, direct. 'You look so tired.'

'Quara!' His lips touched her fingers in old-fashioned greeting, lingering on the smooth surface of her skin. Estar had had skin like that, he remembered. Soft, richly black, unblemished. He caught himself on the edge of nostalgia. Estar was dead and, if the prediction of the machine could be relied on, he would join her wherever the dead waited within a matter of ten Toy days. Five hundred hours, he thought. Thirty-six thousand beats of a human heart. A short enough span in which to do all the things he had so consistently postponed. Too short. To attempt the impossible would be to accomplish nothing.

'I forget myself!' He straightened, smiling, releasing her hand. 'Would you care for tea? Cakes? I have some delicious candied fruits you may care to sample.'

'Thank you, no. Your slave is a charming young girl. She insisted that I have some refreshment. A compote which she said was a favourite of yours.'

'She is young,' he said. 'Eager to please.'

'And perhaps a little jealous?' She

smiled and shook her head. 'Leon, you are too considerate. Your slaves love you too much.' And then, without changing either voice or expression, 'How did the meeting go?'

'Slowly. We had much to discuss.'

'And?'

'Nothing. No decision.'

He felt the impact of her eyes. 'Vohmis called,' she said slowly. 'He told me what you had asked the machine.'

'He should not have done that!' Leon felt a rising wave of anger. 'To abuse privacy so! I have a mind to . . . '

' . . . face him and demand satisfaction?' she said, interrupting. 'To call that poor old man out somewhere and fight him until he bleeds or dies?' Her hand fell to his arm, gripped, shook it a little. 'Leon! Vohmis is a friend. An old friend of us both. He had to call me. He is worried.'

He isn't the only one, thought Leon grimly. He remembered those he had left at the meeting, their horror and refusal to accept what he had told them, their blind panic. They would check, of course; the matter was too grave for them not to do that. But they would learn what he had learned. Gain what he had gained. A temporal shift in an objective viewpoint. But they wouldn't thank him for that. No man likes to know the hour of his death.

'Why?' she demanded. 'Why did you do it?'

He shrugged. 'What else could I do? Mulwo's death proved what you had hinted. The Toymaster has a spy among us. To sit and do nothing was to wait as he cut us down one after the other. We need something to hold us together, bind us close. Frightened men make poor conspirators — unless they are frightened enough. Then they become what conspirators ought to be. Desperate. Willing to take any chance, any risk which promises success. Well, perhaps now they'll do something.'

'And if they don't?'

'They will,' he said positively. 'They must. Our survival instinct is too strong for them not to. Faced with certain death what can they lose?'

'Their pride,' she said bitterly. 'Leon,

men are not as they were. The old days are gone. Now they think more of wealth and comfort than decency and honour. Why else has the Toymaster been permitted to rule as he does? Even the stockholders' meetings have become a farce.' She moved restlessly about the solar, turned, came very close. The scent of her perfume was strong in his nostrils. 'Leon. Must it be this way?'

'Is there another?' Impulsively he gripped her upper arms. *Strange*, he thought, *how the knowledge of imminent death can encourage the use of small familiarities.* 'No,' he said. 'There is no other. But you have nothing to worry about, Quara. This doesn't concern you. It is time the members of the Spinners Association began to act like men: I think they will do it.'

'If they try and fail,' she pointed out, 'the Toymaster will be less than merciful.'

'Another spur,' he agreed.

'Or another reason for running. They are weak,' she said. 'This has been a game to them. Now that it has become real and they scent the odour of blood do you think they will gain strength? You know them,' she insisted. 'Aside from yourself who is strong enough to face the Toymaster?'

His hands fell from the soft roundness of her arms. 'You flatter me,' he said dryly. 'Against your brother I would be fortunate to last more than a minute. But it will not come to that. Commander Gyrn does not believe in the old courtesies. And,' he added, 'I could never challenge the Toymaster. I could never get the necessary stock to make me eligible.'

'You could,' she said impulsively. 'Leon! I could give you mine!'

'No!' He was emphatic in his refusal. 'We have discussed this before. The risk is too great. The Spinners Association will act as a group or die as individuals. There is no other choice.'

'You could leave,' she suggested. 'Get off-world.'

'Run?'

'A word,' she said impatiently. 'Must you die when ships are leaving every day?'

He frowned, reluctant to admit that he had already considered the possibility.

Considered it and decided against it. It would mean leaving everything behind. His dividend could only be spent on Toy. Had he more time he could, perhaps, convert his possessions into portable wealth, jewels, artifacts of high intrinsic value. But he had no time, even if he were permitted to leave with so much.

'You would be alive,' she said shrewdly, guessing his thoughts. 'At least you would be that.'

True, he admitted to himself. But as what? A pauper? He would rather die a Stockholder of Toy.

★　★　★

'More,' said Techon. He leaned forward, eyes narrowed. 'Add another ten pounds.'

Dumarest sweated beneath the strain. He stood, naked but for a snug pair of briefs, pressing hard against the wall of the apparatus. Both arms were extended, hands gripping a bar, muscles standing out on arms, back and shoulders as he fought the pressure. Should he yield the bar would snap forward, stopping just short of his chest, searing his nerves as electrodes made contact. Twice already he had suffered the pain of defeat. It was not an experience he wished to repeat.

'Another ten,' snapped the fightmaster. He rose from his chair, came close to the edge of the apparatus, looked sharply at Dumarest's face as Krul increased the pressure. The sweat was to be expected, the lines of strain, the anger in the eyes. 'The best training devices are often the simplest,' he said conversationally. 'But a man has need of an incentive if he is to do his best. The desire to avoid pain is strong. It is remarkable how much extra effort a man is capable of if he is driven to it.' He raised his voice. 'Add ten.'

The tips of his fingers touched Dumarest's arm, felt the straining quiver beneath the skin.

'A little more,' I think,' he mused. 'Already you have shown a remarkable improvement.' He fell silent, watching, gauging just how much more Dumarest could take. Not much, he decided. He fell back from the straining man. 'Add another five.'

Before Krul could increase the pressure Dumarest acted. He released the bar, ducking so that he dived beneath the vicious snap, springing clear of the platform and escaping the punishing agony. Techon shook his head, his right hand caressing his left wrist. 'Will you never learn? How often must I teach you to obey? You were supposed to withstand the pressure of that bar as long as you could. How else can I determine your full capacity?'

Dumarest glared at the fightmaster. 'Capacity for what? Accepting punishment?' He took one step toward the fightmaster.

And collapsed in a red tide of pain.

Water shocked him back to full awareness. He rose, moisture running down his face, dripping onto the mats beneath his feet. He took a long, shuddering breath, then visibly relaxed. While he wore the collar there was nothing he could do to escape the electronic whip.

'That is better,' said Techon. He came closer, thrust his scarred face into

Dumarest's own. 'Listen,' he snapped. 'I have spent time, trouble and money on you. More than a hundred subjective hours of slow time therapy. The best of training. I've put flesh and muscle on your bones. I am a fair man,' he said. 'I do not ask for gratitude. But I do demand co-operation.'

'I'll co-operate,' said Dumarest.

'Yes,' said Techon softly. 'You'll co-operate or I'll sear your brains with continuous punishment. I'll have you whining, crawling like a dog, begging for release. Think about it, my friend. Here only I am master.'

He looked around the gymnasium. Men were busy at their training, some young, a few old, most scarred with old wounds. They studiously avoided his eyes. Techon nodded, glanced as Dumarest.

'They appreciate the lesson,' he said. 'Now wash and eat. After that we shall continue with your training.'

There was a rough camaraderie in the establishment. Men watched each other's progress with interest, eager to learn, to spot a weakness or strength, never knowing when they would be matched one against the other. But that was not often and, at mealtimes, they could relax.

'You're rubbing the fightmaster the wrong way,' said a man as he helped himself to more food from the pot. It was succulently flavoured, heavy with protein, devoid of fat-producing carbohydrates. Three kinds of fruit and a thin, sharp wine completed the menu. 'Techon isn't too bad when you get to know him.'

Dumarest looked up from his plate. 'Perhaps I don't want to get to know him.'

'Have you any choice?' The man burped, swallowed some wine. 'You're his property,' he reminded. 'His slave. We all are. But things aren't so bad if you play along. Good food, decent beds, a bit of fun now and again.' He winked.

'Techon is worried,' said a man from lower down the table. 'He's got the concession to supply the entertainment at the Toymaster's party on Dividend Day. Our kind of entertainment, that is,' he amended. 'It means a lot to him. If he puts on a good show he'll be made.'

'A lot to him but not to us,' said a man

facing Dumarest. 'We get butchered and he gets the credit.' He reached for the jug of wine. 'Still, that's life.'

'It isn't so bad,' insisted the first speaker. 'I was a fisherman before getting into debt. Have you ever been out on the sea at night? Ice on the decks. The wind cutting right through to the bone. Hard work and small reward. I can make more with a lucky bet than I could in a month.'

Dumarest looked at him. 'Are you allowed to bet?'

'Sure, if you've got the money. In fact the fightmaster encourages it. Gives a fighter that much extra incentive,' he explained. 'You have to back yourself, of course, and to win.' He chuckled. 'Not much good winning a bet if you have to die to do it.' He drank the rest of his wine. 'Well, let's get back to work.'

Techon drove them savagely, viciously, paying special attention to Dumarest. The fisherman explained as they showered after the session.

'You're a special prize. You escaped from the arena. With that sort of reputation the Toymaster will expect something special.

The fightmaster doesn't intend to let him down.'

Dumarest soaped his throat, fingers lingering on the collar. Every man in the establishment wore a similar device. His fingers slipped beneath the flexible band, closed, twisted the metal.

'Don't do that!' said the fisherman sharply. 'You might just be unlucky,' he explained. 'You might manage to break it.'

'That was the idea,' said Dumarest dryly.

'Then forget it. It's loaded with explosive. Unless unlocked with the proper key it will blow your head off break it, cut it, burn it apart and it will do the same. And,' he added, 'if you run off, try to escape, Techon can send a signal to reach you anywhere on Toy.' He touched his own collar, shrugged. 'Well,' he said philosophically, 'it's all a part of the game.'

Your game, thought Dumarest bleakly. *Not mine*. He looked down at his clenched hands. He would never be able to adopt the mental resignation of a slave.

169

High against the dull brown of the slope something moved: an animal, hoofed, horned, blended into the background, its natural fur camouflage making it one with the scenery. Groshen lifted his bow, a thing of metal with a weight of a hundred and twenty pounds, the arrow a feathered shaft of viciously barbed steel. Muscles bulged beneath cloth of silver as he drew slowly on the string.

'Three hundred yards,' he commented. 'Agreed?'

Commander Gyrn shaded his eyes. 'With respect, my lord, fifty yards more.' He wetted a finger, held it to the breeze. 'And, if I may suggest, aim five yards to the right. The wind is stronger on the slopes.'

'You are accustomed to the bow?' Groshen was ironic. 'But of course, I forgot. Were you not a hunter of game before you became a hunter of men?'

Gyrn bowed. 'As you well know, my lord.'

'A poacher on my father's estate. Only

my friendship saved you from the block.' The string gave a deep thrum; the arrow flashed, rose a little, sank deeply into the soil inches from the beast. It started, sprang to a hummock, sprang again. Groshen flung aside the bow and snatched a proffered rifle. He lifted, aimed, fired all in one movement. The animal fell lifeless to the dirt.

'Get it,' snapped Groshen to an attendant. He looked at the rifle in his hands. 'You said five yards,' he accused. 'This should not have been necessary.'

Gyrn swallowed. 'My lord, I was mistaken. It should have been more.'

'Much more.' As if by accident the muzzle of the rifle centred on the commander. 'You judged wrongly, Gyrn. I hope that it is not a habit of yours?'

'No, my lord.'

'Perhaps it would be best for you to cease from making judgments,' suggested the Toymaster softly. 'You see how easily you can be mistaken?'

Gyrn bowed, conscious of the eyes of the attendants, the tall, scarlet figure of the cyber. Creel stood with his back to the wind, hands buried in the wide sleeves of his robe, face shadowed by the cowl. To one side lay the rafts, the appurtenances of the hunt. The clothes of the servitors made bright splotches against the vegetation.

Gay, thought Gyrn. Bright and cheerful, with a picnic-like atmosphere. A strange place for him to make his report, but who could tell the motives of the Toymaster? Had he been summoned merely to be taught a lesson? To be made to look small? To be given a secret instruction?

The latter, he thought, and relaxed. He had nothing to fear. The instruction had already been given. To obey. Not to question but to obey,

Groshen lowered the rifle, stepped closer, the wind tearing his words. 'You have something to report?'

'Yes, my lord. Of the Spinners Association four are now dead. Mulwo, Restern and two others. They . . . '

'Name them,' snapped the Toymaster. 'Explain.'

'Keen and Wylie, my lord. They were

detained when attempting to book passage off-world. It was discovered that both sought to export items of high intrinsic value. They protested, struggled and were unfortunately shot while attempting to avoid arrest.'

Groshen nodded.

'As regards the matter of their stock,' said Gyrn carefully. 'It . . . '

' . . . will revert to their heirs,' snapped the Toymaster. 'You know the law. A man's family cannot be disenfranchised. However,' he said slowly, 'there are grounds to extract a heavy fine.' He smiled at the commander. 'I haven't forgotten, Gyrn. You shall have ten per cent of whatever extra stock I obtain.'

'Thank you, my lord.'

'You may go.' Groshen stared after the commander as he walked to his raft, then closed the distance between himself and Creel. 'Your prediction has proved itself correct,' he said. 'Already they try to run.'

'It was an obvious move, my lord. The landing field is sealed?'

'Yes.'

'Then you must anticipate concerted

action against yourself by those that remain,' said the cyber evenly. 'Desperate men will go to desperate lengths. It is possible they may be tempted to employ an assassin.'

Groshen was contemptuous. 'Let them. How can they hope to succeed?'

They couldn't, thought Creel. The Toymaster's fantastic dividend enabled him to build and maintain a wall of guards, electronic devices, barriers through which no assassin could hope to penetrate. But it was as well to make the suggestion, to allow the Toymaster to underestimate his intelligence a little. The man was still adamant in his refusal to allow the Cyclan to provide its services. Still insistent that, because of the Library, he could do without any other aid.

'I was not wholly thinking of the possibility of an assassin,' he admitted. 'I mentioned it, that is all. There is another, far stronger danger.'

'Which is?'

Creel remained silent.

'I asked you a question, cyber. I am not accustomed to being ignored.' Anger flared the Toymaster's nostrils. His knuckles showed taut where he gripped the rifle. 'Do I have to make you answer?'

'You could not.' Creel spoke nothing but the truth. 'But, my lord, surely the Library could give you the same information?'

'Possibly,' admitted the Toymaster. 'But the Library does not volunteer predictions and suggestions. It has to be asked.' He relaxed, smiling. 'You have made your point, cyber. I shall bear it in mind when I come to make my decision regarding your offer. And now?'

Transparent, thought Creel. A mental child despite his arrogance, so quickly had he snatched the bait. And yet not so much a child that he was without natural cunning. No ruler could be without that.

'I spoke of your enemies planning concerted action,' Creel said in his even modulation. 'It is something to be considered. Study of the regulations and Original Law shows that there is a way in which they could, perhaps, best you.'

'A challenge?' Groshen laughed, white teeth flashing against the red of his throat.

'Impossible! To do that they need to acquire more stock. They haven't enough.'

'Perhaps not,' said Creel. 'But your sister, the Lady Quara, has.'

'Quara?' Groshen frowned, thoughtful. 'She wouldn't,' he decided. 'She is too selfish for that. Why should she seek to destroy me?' He looked down at the rifle in his hand. 'Unless Hurl . . . ?'

'A wise man takes precautions against every dangerous possibility,' urged Creel. 'No matter how remote it may seem. Your sister is your greatest danger. Alone she holds the means to destroy you. Why take a needless risk?'

Groshen scowled. 'Are you suggesting that I kill her? The child of my father? My sister in blood?'

'There are other ways. For example, it is not unknown for brother to marry sister. On many worlds it is the custom among those who rule.' He caught the expression on Groshen's face. 'Or, perhaps, you could gain her stock in other ways. A wager, perhaps? I give you the conception, my lord. I can do no more.'

It was enough. Greed and ambition

went hand in hand. Her stock added to his would make him inviolate, A little more and he would have the majority percentage. Then he would literally control the destiny of the planet. Toy would become his personal plaything.

Groshen stretched, laughing, deep echoes rolling from the slopes. 'I'll do it, cyber. Tonight, at the Dividend Day party. Within a month I'll be the absolute ruler of this world. Then, my friend, I will show men how to rule.'

8

Dividend Day and all Toy threw a party. The festivities began as the sun died. The streets glowed with coloured lights, musicians ignored the cold as they led lines of singing dancers in tortuous patterns. Fires blazed and animals were roasted whole. Wine gushed from the fountains, kept warm and potable by electronic heat. Gaudy weaves, grotesque masks, laughter and loving ruled as the stockholders celebrated their new acquisition of wealth. It had been a good dividend; they could afford to be generous. As the night chilled the streets would empty but within the houses the party would last until dawn.

At the palace the Toymaster had invited selected guests to share his fun. They sat around a sunken enclosure, slaves running with sweetmeats and wine, titbits and sprays of refreshing perfume. Guards stood motionless, statues in the flaring light of scented flambeaux. Pipes, drums and cymbals stirred the air together with nerve-tingling sonics and electronic stimulants. Each female guest had been given a gift.

A girl shrieked as she opened her package and saw the flash of jewels. Another echoed the scream as a crawling insect, as large as her hand, scuttled over her lap in a frantic search for darkness. A woman, more cautious, probed her package, felt a resistance. Looking up, she met Groshen's eyes. She thinned her lips and pressed, burst the sac. Liquid vileness fouled her hand — but within the sac rested a diamond.

'Wine!' The Toymaster was enjoying himself, the success of his practical jokes. 'A toast,' he commanded. 'To Toy!'

They drank.

'Another!' He waited as slaves refilled the goblets. 'To a record dividend!'

They drank again.

'One more toast!' He stared at them with mocking eyes. 'To me. To the master of Toy.'

For the third time their goblets were

emptied. It made a good foundation, he thought, for the success of the evening. Quara was noted for her ability to carry wine. All he had to do was get her high enough, angry enough and the rest would be automatic. Hot words such as they had exchanged a thousand times before in family quarrels. But tonight she would be speaking to the Toymaster, not to her brother.

Groshen turned, looking to where a scarlet shape sat like a living flame in the dancing light of the flambeaux. Who had need of a cyber when he could use his own cunning? When he had sucked Creel dry he would send him packing. Until then let him sit and wait and hope to ensnare another fish in his net. It would not be the fish of Toy.

He leaned to where Quara sat. 'More wine, my sister? Come, this is a time for celebration.' He looked past her to where Leon sat at her side. 'Drink up, Stockholder. Have you nothing to celebrate?'

Passively Leon allowed a slave to replenish his goblet. He lifted it, sipped, eyes direct as he stared at Groshen. 'I drink,' he said. 'To the death of friends and the abuse of privilege.'

He felt the girl tense at his side. Reflected light shone from the Toymaster's eyes, his teeth, filling sockets and mouth with the colour of blood.

'You are a brave man, Stockholder Hurl. Or a foolish one.'

'Just a man,' said Leon evenly. He lowered his left hand. Only Quara was armed, the inevitable poniard in her belt, more a decoration than a weapon, but it had a point and could kill. To snatch it, thrust it deep into Groshen's throat, to kill the man while he had the chance. After all, what had he to lose? Then the Toymaster leaned back, safely out of reach, and the moment had passed.

The music rose as dancers swept into the enclosure, naked bodies shining with oil, men and women depicting an age-old ritual in stylised formation, merging, parting, uniting in coordinated frenzy.

Leon felt Quara's hand on his thigh. 'You wanted to kill him,' she whispered. 'I read your face.'

181

He nodded,

'You would have died trying. He is fast, Leon, trained. Don't let him goad you into throwing away your life.'

'Is it so valuable? Now?'

'To me, yes. And you are not dead yet, Leon. We can still hope.'

Hope, he thought dully. *Hope for what? A miracle?* He glanced at the circle of rapt faces, beyond them to the statuesque guards, past them to the hanging weaves. *A trap*, he thought suddenly. *I'm in a trap. Quara was right. It is a time for caution.*

The dancers ended their performance, bowed, scrabbled for the coins flung at their feet. The music broke, recommenced with a solemn beat. Fightmaster Techon strode before the assembly.

'My lord!' He bowed to the Toymaster. 'Gentles one and all.' His gesture included the rest. 'With respect to your pleasure a small entertainment. A diversion which I trust you will not find unamusing.'

He bowed again, backed from the enclosure. Naked men, oiled, sprang in view, muscles rippling as they grappled, each trying to throw the other. The preliminary, Leon knew, to more violent events.

Groshen spoke from where he sat. 'A wager, sister? Ten units of stock on the one with the white skin.' He waited. 'No? Then you, Stockholder Hurl? Will you take my bet?'

Leon nodded, too disinterested to argue. Again he felt the warning pressure on his thigh.

'Be careful, Leon,' whispered Quara. She leaned forward, pretending an interest, turning her face from Groshen's watching eyes. 'Do not wager too much. And,' she added quickly, 'do not tell me that it does not matter now. The Toymaster has some plan, I am sure of it. I know him too well to doubt.'

The bout ended with Groshen the winner. Others followed. Two men fought with spiked gloves. Another two with vicious maces. A man with a sword was paired with another armed with a quarterstaff. The match was ridiculously uneven; the swordsman didn't stand a chance and Leon won heavily from the Toymaster.

'More wine!' ordered Groshen as the contenders left the enclosure. 'A toast to your victory, Stockholder Hurl.' He gestured to a slave, pointed at his sister's empty goblet. 'Come, Quara, you cannot refuse to toast our old friend. Our very old friend,' he repeated meaningfully. 'He knew our mother . . . perhaps too well.'

Leon looked down. His hand was tight around his goblet, the wine slopping as he fought the temptation to throw it in the Toymaster's face. To talk so of Estar!

'To you, Leon!' Quara drank hastily, determined to avoid a quarrel between the two men. Angrily she glared at her brother. 'Must you mention our mother? Have you no pride?'

Groshen smiled, reached out and helped himself to a titbit from a tray. The smoked fish dressed with sharp sauce rested tantalisingly on the tongue. Slowly he chewed, swallowed, savouring the moment. Now? A little more pressure and Quara would explode. He knew her temper too well. Now?

Drums thundered, insistent, demanding, claiming attention for the next bout. Groshen reached for another titbit. Quara could wait.

*   *   *

It was familiar, the men, the scent of oil and sweat, the little sounds, a cough, the rustle of movement, the thin, spiteful rasp of a whetted blade. Dumarest had known it all before. Only the collar was different, that and his status. Never before had he fought as a slave. For money, yes. For dangerous sport against all contenders with a prize at stake and the money going to the one who drew first blood. But not this deliberately managed slaughter for the titivation of a jaded crowd.

Facing him, the fisherman tried to smile. 'It's the luck of the draw, Earl. It could have been anyone. It had to be you.'

Dumarest made no comment. Beyond the door he could hear the cheers and laughter of those who watched as men tried to kill each other.

'You're fast,' said the fisherman. 'Too fast. Maybe we could arrange something?' He lowered his voice. 'I don't mind taking a cut or two. Somewhere yielding lots of blood.' He spat. 'That's what they want out there. Blood and a lot of it.'

'We could refuse to fight,' suggested Dumarest.

'We could,' agreed the man. 'But what would Techon do then?' He touched his collar. 'We would still provide a spectacle. I've seen it happen. I know.' His big hands knotted, clenched where they rested on his bare knees, moved uneasily over the skin. He was, Dumarest thought, either afraid or putting on an act. He sat silent, waiting.

'Listen,' said the fisherman abruptly. 'Let's play it smart. We could play around for a while, plenty of footwork and blade-clashing; you know how it's done. Make it look good. Then I'll come in low and aiming up. You block and touch my ear. Slit the lobe. It's a minor wound but bleeds a lot.' He looked anxious. 'Understand?'

Dumarest nodded. 'And?'

186

'We keep it up. Maybe you'll let me make a hit. A touch on the shoulder, maybe, or on the side. Nothing serious but looking good. Then you touch me again. After a while I drop. Techon won't like it, but so what? We'll both be alive.'

Dumarest doubted it. Such an arrangement would leave him wide open for an easy kill if the fisherman decided to go for it. And he would so decide. He'd be a fool to do anything else.

Techon came bustling to where they sat. The fightmaster was sweating, his scarred face betraying his agitation. 'All right, you,' he snapped at the fisherman. 'You go on next. Knives and make it good.' His hand fell on Dumarest's shoulder as he made to rise. 'Not you. You're being saved for something special!'

'Such as?'

Techon sat in the place the fisherman had vacated. 'I don't like it,' he admitted. 'I'm a fair man and I like a fair match. But what can you do against the Toymaster? You escaped the arena,' he said. 'You were on his side — and his side lost. According to him you should have died with the rest.'

Dumarest looked at the man. 'So?'

Techon didn't answer, cocking his head so as to hear the noise from the enclosure. There was a burst of laughter, a yell of applause. 'That didn't last long,' he said, and hesitated. 'Look,' he said. 'I worked for a webmaster once. Most men panic, they sweat fear. They get bitten and it slows them down to the point where they can't move. They know everything that's going on but they can't do a thing about it. So don't panic and don't get bitten.' He rose. 'Come on.'

'You're trying to tell me something,' said Dumarest. 'What?'

'You'll find out. Now get on your feet and move!' Techon dropped his right hand to his left wrist. 'Don't make me use this,' he said. 'Not now.'

Dumarest stood up, walked with the fightmaster to the door opening onto the enclosure. It opened. A hand thrust at his back to push him forward. He took three steps, then halted, staring at what lay ahead.

A wire-mesh cage, twelve feet square,

ten high, fitted with rotating doors at either end, panels of mesh which permitted entry. Tied to one of the doors, naked, his big-nosed face reflecting his terror, was Legrain. He looked at Dumarest.

'They got me,' he said. 'The guards grabbed me at dusk. It looks as if we're going to end the same way together after all.'

Dumarest looked past him at the contents of the cage. A dozen weavers crawled in restless anticipation. Spiders used to eating raw, living meat. Starved. Eager to feed. Hands caught his arms, lifted him, carried him to where the Toymaster sat on the raised platform above.

Groshen took a sip of wine.

'You fought for me and lost,' he said. 'Therefore you deserve to die. But you were not alone.' He gestured toward Legrain. 'Now you will fight again, not for me but for yourself. Yourself and your friend,' he amended. 'On your prowess depends both your lives.' He paused, sipping wine, eyes watchful over the rim

189

of the goblet. It had been a good touch to make the man not only fight for himself but for his friend also. 'Is there anything you wish to say?'

'Yes,' said Dumarest. 'Am I to be permitted a weapon?'

'You have a weapon,' said the Toymaster. 'Yourself. Your skill, your cunning, your ferocity against those of the weavers.'

Dumarest flexed his hands. It had been a hopeless request but he'd had to ask. His eyes raised, drifting over the watching faces. A woman stared at him, dressed in brilliant green, emeralds in her hair. Beside her a man, older, clenched his hand on a goblet of wine as if it were the throat of an enemy. Behind them, like a menacing flame, he recognised the scarlet robe of a cyber.

Groshen slammed down his goblet. 'Begin!'

Dumarest shrugged aside the reaching hands of the guards and walked to the vacant door. He mounted the platform, stood looking at the circle of faces, the avid eyes. A click, a sudden movement and he had spun one hundred and eighty degrees. At the far end of the cage Legrain sagged in his bonds. Between them scurried twenty pieces of living nightmare. Dumarest blurred into action.

Chitin crunched beneath a foot. Mandibles clashed as he seized scrabbling legs, lifted, slammed the arachnid onto one of its fellows, crushing them both. He jumped aside as hooked claws raked his back, stamped, felt the legs fracture. Something dropped from the wire roof of the cage. He caught it, flung it against a wall, ran to where Legrain hung, the target for two of the weavers. One fell as Dumarest ripped at its legs. The other scuttled up the wire, falling as he buried his fist in its body.

Desperately he tore at Legrain's bonds.

'Earl! You haven't got time!'

'Shut up! Watch, warn if they get too close.' He grunted as he freed an arm, turned, springing high to land on fragile limbs. *Smash their legs*, he thought. *Immobilize them. Stay clear of their venom. And move fast. Fast!*

He heard a shout, jumped back in time to save Legrain, added another to the pile of twitching bodies. He stooped, tore at the lashings holding the other man's legs, rose, gripped his tied arm, jerked. The lashing broke as a weight landed on his shoulders. He whirled, reaching back, feeling the claw of legs, the rasp of a hairy abdomen. Mandibles tore at his hair as he gripped, lifted, swung over his head and to the floor. Pain stabbed his left ankle. He punched down at the glitter of eyes, chopped at legs, kicked himself free.

Ooze slimed his body, foul, nauseating in its smell. Legrain shouted, flailed desperately, yelled as a weaver tore at his flesh. Dumarest raced towards him, fought the numbing agony of his leg, thinking only of the necessity to kill, to smash, to destroy and keep on destroying.

And, suddenly, there was nothing. Nothing but the litter of bodies, the circle of faces, the frantic, yelling, screaming roar of cheers.

Quara was on her feet, her heart pounding with excitement, cheering with the rest. She turned, gripped Leon by the arm. 'He did it! He beat the Toymaster! He won!'

'Yes,' said Leon. He felt ill, nauseated at the sight, nostrils filled with the dry, acrid stench of the weavers. But that was imagination, he knew. Their scent could not penetrate the perfume scenting the air.

'Fast,' said Quara, resuming her seat. 'So fast.' She stared at the cage, the two men, at Dumarest where he leaned against the wire. His chest heaved, his face was taut with pain. One leg lifted, barely touching the ground. 'He's been bitten. They both have.'

'That isn't surprising,' said Leon. 'The weavers move quickly when they sense food. They . . . ' He broke off, eyes narrowed as men entered the enclosure and busied themselves about the cage. 'Vogel! What are you doing here?'

The webmaster turned, saw Leon, approached. 'The orders of the Toymaster, Stockholder Hurl. He gave me the task of supplying the weavers. But they weren't good stock,' he reassured. 'I only picked the intractable ones, the rogues, those who would not learn. There's been no waste, Stockholder.'

'Why was I not informed?'

Vogel turned sullen. 'It was the order of the Toymaster, Stockholder, How could I refuse?'

How indeed? thought Leon grimly. He looked to where Groshen sat, scowling, obviously annoyed. *Had it come to this so soon? Had a man no rights?* He looked at the webmaster. 'What is to happen now?'

'We clean out the cage and restock it, Stockholder. I have still a score of weavers unused.'

'You mean those men are to fight again?' Quara leaned forward, eyes blazing. 'I will not allow it! Treat the pair of them to neutralise the venom. At once!'

Vogel hesitated, his eyes drifting from her face to Leon's, from his to the Toymaster's. *A man trapped,* thought Leon. *Not sure as to where his duty lies.* He felt himself tense with anger. The man should have had no question of doubt. 'You heard Stockholder Quara Groshen,' he said coldly. 'It is my order that she be obeyed. Immediately!'

Again Vogel looked at the Toymaster.

Groshen leaned forward, his voice a feral purr. 'Is there trouble, Stockholder Hurl?'

Leon met his eyes. 'No,' he said shortly. 'I am merely giving my webmaster his orders.'

'He has his orders.'

'Not from me,' insisted Leon. 'Those men will not fight again.'

'Indeed?' Groshen lifted his goblet, sipped a little wine. 'And if I should say they will?'

Rebellion, thought Leon. *He's driving me to open defiance and, when I do, he will call it rebellion.* His eyes left the Toymaster, drifted around the circle of watching faces. 'We are your guests, Toymaster,' he said, forcing a smile. 'But I put it to the others. Should these men fight again?'

Their negative came in a shout. Leon relaxed a little. The strain runs true, he thought. Those who had descended from the original settlers still admired courage and could respect bravery. A shower of money fell to the floor of the enclosure, reward for a good performance. Abruptly the Toymaster nodded. 'As you will,' he said loudly. 'Now, a toast to a brave man!'

They drank as attendants dismantled the cage and removed the parts. Vogel was busy with the two men, cleansing their wounds and neutralizing the spider-venom; others were picking up the money, cleaning the space for the next event.

Groshen lowered his emptied goblet. A scarlet shadow stooped, whispered in his ear.

'My lord,' said Creel. 'A suggestion. Would it not be as well if those two men were matched one against the other?'

The Toymaster pondered.

'They are friends,' whispered the cyber. 'Need I say more?'

He retreated to his seat, face a pale, ruby-stained blotch in the shadow of his cowl, hands buried in his wide sleeves. Thoughtfully Groshen held out his goblet for more wine.

The cyber was wrong, of course; it would not be a good match and certainly it wouldn't be a popular bout. His guests wouldn't like it and the men might even refuse to fight. But still the suggestion held merit. He looked at Quara over the rim of his goblet, at Leon seated beside her. Twice had things almost come to a head. The third time would be the last.

He leaned forward, looked at his sister. 'When men are paid to win or die, and do neither, what then?'

She hesitated, sensing a trap, not knowing what to say.

'You, Stockholder Hurl?' Groshen's eyes moved to Leon. 'In such a case what would you suggest?'

Leon shook his head. 'I don't know, Stockholder.'

'The answer of a coward,' said Groshen bitingly. 'I am not so afraid. The answer, of course, is to kill them both.'

'I disagree,' said Leon. 'A brave man is worthy of respect.'

'Perhaps,' admitted the Toymaster. 'You know,' he said casually. 'I often wonder why my mother refused your hand. Could it have been that she found you lacking in the qualities which command respect?'

Leon took a deep, shuddering breath, 'You are saying?'

'I am calling you a coward, Stockholder

197

Hurl. Do I make it plain enough? A coward!'

Quara thrust out a hand, knocked aside the goblet Leon had lifted, sent the wine spilling into the enclosure instead of into the Toymaster's face. This, she thought, was what Groshen had wanted. To goad Leon to the point where he would lose his self-control, strike, suffer death as an immediate consequence.

Angrily she faced her brother. 'You!' she said. 'To talk of cowardice! How many guards defend you, my dear brother? How many men fight your battles? Could you do as that man did?' She gestured toward Dumarest. 'Have you the courage to match your own skin against someone stronger than a ten-year-old girl?'

His eyes blazed, matching her own. 'Careful, sister!'

'Why? Because you are afraid of me? Afraid that I'll tell everyone the truth? You're rotten, Groshen. Mentally sick. Decadent. Why else these blood-sports? This filth?'

He rose, tall, overwhelming. 'Enough!'

'Enough,' she jeered. 'Can't you even stand the impact of words? Do you intend hitting me to stop my mouth?' She rose to face him, magnificent in her rage. 'Hit me, then! I dare you to hit me!'

He smiled. 'Very well, my sister. I accept your challenge.'

'No!' Leon sprang to his feet. *A trap,* he thought wildly. *All the time it has been a trap. I guessed it but didn't guess for whom. Not for me, but for her.* 'You cannot,' he said quickly to the Toymaster. 'No challenge was issued.'

'I think there was,' said Groshen smoothly. 'I think all present will agree with me. I have been dared to strike. If that is not a challenge, what is?' He smiled even wider. 'And,' he pointed out, 'she is perfectly eligible to make such a challenge. She holds the necessary stock as set out in Original Law.'

Leon shook his head. 'No,' he said again, desperately. 'She . . . ' He broke off as Quara laid her hand gently across his lips.

'Do not beg,' she said. 'The thing is done.'

199

'But it was a trap. Can't you see that? He has deliberately led you into this.' He appealed to the Toymaster. 'You can't fight a woman. Certainly not your own sister.'

'Do you offer to take her place?' Groshen gave a careless shrug. 'I have no objection to her use of a proxy.' His eyes held sadistic mirth as he looked at the stockholder. 'Two, if she wishes.'

Quara reached out, caught Leon by the arm pulled him close. 'You mean that?'

'Certainly.' The Toymaster didn't trouble to hide his contempt. 'But you will have a hard time finding another such as Leon. Not all men are willing to throw away their lives for the memory of a pretty face.'

That is true, thought Leon sickly. *To face the Toymaster is to invite death.* He writhed against the invisible jaws of the trap that had sprung on them both. He could not let Quara fight, but what real good could he do by taking her place? *None*, he told himself bitterly. *You can die and that is all.*

9

Legrain paced the floor, scowling, obviously ill at ease, 'I don't like it,' he said. 'First the guards grab me, put me in that cage, then they bring me here. Why?' he demanded. 'Why didn't they just let me go? I've done nothing wrong. Aside from staying alive, that is,' he said sombrely. 'To the Toymaster that's a crime.'

Dumarest made no comment. He sat in a form-fitting chair, booted feet resting on the thick carpet. He had been bathed, fed, given his own clothes, brought to this house and left to wait. He didn't know why. But he was still a slave. His fingers touched the collar around his throat. He was still that.

'Why?' demanded Legrain again. 'Why bring me here? What's it all about?'

'You'll find out soon enough,' said Dumarest. He leaned back and studied the ceiling. It was covered with painted reliefs depicting old battles, struggles, wars of men against men and men against beasts. He lowered his eyes. To one side tall windows glowed with morning light. Low pedestals supported odd shapes of fused glass shining with colourful brilliance. The air carried the scent of flowers.

A door opened. A servant came forward and beckoned to Dumarest. 'You may go in now,' she said. And to Legrain, 'Not you. You are to wait here.'

The door opened into a smaller room, a study, Dumarest guessed from the books lining the walls, the wide desk, the compact recording equipment. It was deserted. A stellar chart hung against a wall, a projector beside it with a rack of recordings. The chart was a superimposed three-dimensional representation, hard to make out without the selective viewer, the colour-planes tending to merge and dissolve one into the other.

Dumarest was frowning over it when there was a click, a panel slid aside and Quara entered the room. She stood smiling as the door slid closed behind her. 'Are you interested in astronomy?'

'Yes, my lady.'

'It was a foolish question.' She crossed the room towards him, stood close enough for him to smell the perfume of her hair. 'You are a traveller. As such you are bound to have an interest in the stars.' She laughed a little. 'You must excuse me; I am not usually stupid.'

Dumarest looked down at her from the vantage of his height. 'I would not have called you stupid, my lady,' he said slowly. 'A little headstrong, perhaps.'

'You heard? At the party, after you fought the weavers, you heard?'

'Yes, my lady. I must thank you for what you did. I do not think I could have won another bout,' he said honestly.

'The weavers?' She shrugged. 'It was Leon who stopped the Toymaster, not I. You should thank him. But you heard what passed between me and my brother?'

'A challenge was issued,' he said. 'And accepted. Much to your surprise,' he said shrewdly. 'I think, my lady, that you were led into a trap.'

'I was,' she admitted. 'And I was too

stupid not to see it.' She pointed to a cabinet. 'In there you will find wine. Pour two glasses.' She watched as he obeyed, took one of the brimming goblets, gestured to a chair. 'Sit. Drink your wine.'

It was tart, refreshingly pleasant, innocently potent. Dumarest looked at the girl. 'My lady is most generous.'

'Your lady is a mess!' Quara set down her glass. 'Do you know anything of the economics of Toy? It is a corporate world,' she continued, not waiting for an answer. 'Every original settler was a shareholder. In theory the system works perfectly. All share in the wealth of the planet. The dividend credit cannot be accumulated, so a constant stream of money is in circulation, thus providing work and expansion. Exports ensure a check on inflation and a market for our surplus.' She snatched up her glass, drank, set it down half empty.

'For a while the system worked and then the inevitable happened. First outside labour came to the planet, men who had no real share in the economy, and thus a hereditary aristocracy grew up.

Then greed reared its head. More stockholders wanted larger amounts of stock. There were struggles, challenges, manoeuvrings for power. In such a situation those that have the most get more. The Toymaster has always had the most.' She shrugged, impatient with explanation. 'Enough of details. At the moment the situation is this — the Toymaster holds forty per cent of stock. I hold ten. If he beats me he will take it. A little more and he will hold the controlling interest,' She paused, eyes hard, lines marring the soft contours of her face. 'You have seen my brother,' she said flatly. 'Suffered at his hands. Would you like to see any world in the absolute power of such a man?'

Dumarest sipped a little wine. 'If you win, my lady,' he said carefully; 'will you not have the same power?'

'Yes,' she admitted. 'But I shall not keep it. Half will be disbursed.' She read his expression. 'Not because I'm an altruist but for the good of Toy. Too few hold too much power. As majority shareholder I can issue new stock — in

205

effect halve the value of what each now holds. It will give millions who now own nothing a chance to share in the communal wealth.'

'And they will work all the harder because of it,' said Dumarest shrewdly. 'But, my lady, with respect, what has this to do with me?'

'Everything,' she said. 'I want you to act as my champion.'

Come, fight and die for me! And that, thought Dumarest, was exactly what she was saying. He stared thoughtfully at the surface of his wine. It was rose-pink, tiny bubbles rising to burst in transient beauty, leaving a ring of temporary rainbows.

'You can fight,' she said. 'The way you beat the weavers showed that.' She frowned. 'How did you beat them? Never before has a man escaped from the pens.'

'The weavers are mutated spiders,' said Dumarest. 'Nothing more. They do not have the skill and intelligence of a man nor do they have his striking power. Only their appearance is disturbing. In my travels I have met many forms of life.' He shrugged. 'Perhaps I was lucky, my lady. I managed to avoid panic.'

She was direct. 'Do you think you could beat the Toymaster?'

'In equal combat? Perhaps.' Dumarest frowned at his wine. 'I do not know, my lady. So many things can happen. It would be best for you to find someone else.'

'Who? There isn't anyone. The Toymaster thought I intended to use Leon as my proxy. The man who stood at my side,' she explained. 'Before witnesses I made him agree to let me use two men to fight for me — I did not say who they would be.' Her lips thinned spitefully. 'It was my turn to lead him into a trap. But it was a small victory,' she admitted. 'Useless unless you agree to act on my behalf.' Dumarest remained silent.

Quara stooped, opened a drawer in the desk, removed a sheet of paper and a small key. She placed them both on the desk and sat down facing Dumarest. 'I have bought you from Techon,' she said abruptly. 'You are now my slave.'

His hand rose, touched the collar

around his neck.

'You do not like being a slave,' she said softly, understanding the gesture. 'Well, let us bargain. I need your help. In return I offer your freedom and wealth enough for you to travel to a dozen stars. The cost of a score of high passages or, if you prefer, enough stock for you to live comfortably on Toy.'

'The alternative, my lady?'

'I return you to the fightmaster.'

Their eyes met, locked as each tried to gauge the determination of the other. Abruptly Dumarest said, 'You do not offer enough, my lady.'

Inwardly she relaxed. He had agreed in principle; all else was a matter of detail. Now it was time for her to be generous, but first she had to be sure. 'You will act for me?'

'You give me little choice,' he said dryly. 'But I need more than you offer.'

'A moment.' She rose, picked up the key, moved to stand behind him. A soft click and the collar was free. She dropped the gleaming length of flexible metal on the sheet of paper, added the key, pushed the little pile toward Dumarest. 'This is your certificate of manumission,' she explained. 'The key and collar you may wish to retain as souvenirs.' She watched as he put the items in a pocket. 'Now we can talk as free people. What more do you demand?'

'Information, my lady.'

She frowned, not understanding.

'The use of the Library,' he said. 'There is something I need to know. The whereabouts of the planet Earth.' He saw her expression. 'I know the name sounds ridiculous but there is such a planet. A bleak place scarred with old wars. I was born on it. I would like your help to find it.'

She rose, crossed to the cabinet, refilled their glasses. 'You came from it,' she said thoughtfully. 'A ship must have carried you. Surely you could retrace your steps?'

'I was very young at the time,' he said. 'A child of ten, alone, more than a little desperate. I stowed away on a ship. The captain should have evicted me, but he was kinder than I deserved. He was old and had no son.' He paused, thinking, eyes clouded with memories. He drank some wine.

'I've been travelling ever since. Deeper and deeper towards the centre, where inhabited worlds are thickest. Among people to whom the planet Earth isn't even a legend.'

'And you came to Toy for what purpose?'

'To consult the Library. A hope,' he said. 'Maybe a wild one but still a hope, Earth doesn't lie in the centre. The stars are not as I remember. It must lie somewhere towards the edge of the galaxy. Certainly where the stars are few. There was a moon,' he said. 'Big, pocked, looking like a rotting fruit as it swung across the sky.'

'Many worlds have moons.'

'And many worlds have men,' he said. 'Have you never thought, my lady, from where they came?'

'From the ground,' she said quickly. 'Carried by ships as we came to Toy from Grail. One world settles the next and so on.'

'Then isn't it possible that all men originated from one world?'

She laughed, amused at the conception. 'My friend, how big a world that must be! Does all grass originate from the same place? All trees, all animals, the fish in the seas and the birds in the air? And are all men alike, as they surely would be if all came from one planet?' She laid her hand on his, black against white. 'See? And there are men with brown skins and yellow. Are they the same as me? Are you the same as me?'

'Yes, my lady. Basically the same. Most men and women can interbreed.'

'Most,' she said quickly, 'but not all. How do you explain that?'

'Mutation, perhaps? A divergence from the main stock?' Dumarest picked up his wine, admitting defeat. She would never be convinced, and how could he blame her? The observable facts were all against what he had claimed could be the truth. Could be. Even he had no way to be certain. 'But is it a bargain, lady? I will be permitted to consult the computer?'

'I will personally give the order to Vohmis.' She tapped the rim of her glass against his own. 'To our victory!'

They drank. Dumarest frowned. 'A moment, my lady. You gained permission to use two men as your proxy. Who is the other?'

'Who else but the man in the cage with you?'

'Legrain?'

'He escaped from the arena. He is your friend.' Her eyes searched his face. 'You object?'

'No, my lady. But will he agree?'

'He has.' She smiled. 'Leon spoke to him while you waited in here alone. He is quite willing to act with you as my proxy.' Again she rapped the edge of her glass against his own, the half-empty goblets ringing like distant bells. 'Come, my friend, let us finish the wine. To victory!'

'To victory,' echoed Dumarest, and added, 'to what it will bring.'

* * *

Outside, in the ornate room, Legrain waited in a fever of impatience. He caught Dumarest by the arm. 'Well, Earl, did you agree?'

212

Dumarest nodded and led the way towards the door. Outside the air was warm with rising heat, the lower windows unshuttered, people thronging the sidewalks still enjoying the euphoria of Dividend Day.

'I thought you'd agree,' said Legrain as they strode along. 'I told that man, Stockholder Hurl, that you would. Did they offer you a good price?'

'Freedom,' said Dumarest shortly. 'That was good enough.'

'Nothing else?' Legrain frowned. 'You should have stuck them,' he said. 'They were desperate. You could have got anything you asked.'

'After the fight,' said Dumarest.

Legrain nodded. 'Well, sure,' he said. 'That was understood. No fight no pay.' He chuckled. 'You know, Earl, it's going to be wonderful. Plenty of money, a fine house, slaves maybe. All I've ever wanted.'

Dumarest turned a corner. 'So you're going for the stock.'

'That's right. Stockholder Legrain. Sounds good, doesn't it? Nothing to do but spend my dividend. No worries about the future. No more fights or hiring myself out to get killed. I may even get married and raise a family. Why not?'

Dumarest didn't answer.

'We could meet up at times,' continued Legrain. 'Live close. Share things. At least we'd have something in common.' He paused, looked around. 'Where are we going?'

'To the landing field.'

'But why?' Legrain looked puzzled. 'What's out there? Look,' he said. 'We should be making plans, working out techniques. That Toymaster's a tough customer. He'll kill us if he can, you know that?'

'I know it,' said Dumarest. He paused at an intersection, continued striding along the sidewalk. The landing field was close. Soon they could see the wire of the fence, the guards, the graceful ships beyond. Even as they watched one lifted, rising with the magic of its Erhaft field, heading toward space and the stars.

Legrain stared after it, shook his head. 'It gets you,' he admitted. 'Every time I see a ship leave I've the urge to follow it.

I guess that's what makes a traveller. But no more. My roving days are over. I'm here to stay.'

'I'm not,' said Dumarest.

Legrain frowned. 'I don't get you, Earl.'

'You don't? It's simple enough.' Dumarest touched his bare throat. 'Now that I've got rid of the collar there's nothing to keep me here. I've credit enough for a Low passage. With what you've got plus the money thrown at us during the party you should have the same. Let's go and find a handler.'

'Are you serious?'

Dumarest frowned. 'What's the matter with you? Do you want to stay here and get yourself killed? And for what? So some spoiled bitch can get even richer?' He shook his head. That's not for me. 'I'm getting out of here while I've got the chance.'

Legrain caught his arm. 'Earl, you can't!' He swallowed. 'The money. Unless we fight we don't get paid.'

'And we won't get killed either,' pointed out Dumarest.

'But . . . '

'What's Toy to you? Just another world,' Dumarest gestured towards the landing field. 'Any one of those ships will take us to another planet. Let's get moving while we've got the chance.'

'No,' said Legrain. He stood, mantled in an odd pride. 'I can't. I've given my word and I can't back down.'

'Don't be a fool, Legrain. Can't you see they're using you?'

Legrain was stubborn. 'Maybe they are but that isn't the point. I made a bargain with them and so did you. We can't let them down, Earl. We just can't do that.'

'No,' said Dumarest quietly. 'I guess we can't.'

* * *

In the drifting cloud of steam a man called out sharply, his voice shrill with pain. Another voice, deeper, answered with a laugh. Something blurred through the air to land with a heavy crash. Sycophantic voices hurried to offer congratulations. 'A wonderful throw, Toymaster!'

'I've never seen a more masterful manoeuvre!'

'The way you weakened him before taking the final grip!'

Commander Gyrn smiled sourly. *Dogs*, he thought. *Yapping at the heels of their master. Weaklings sheltering in his strength, eager and willing to turn, one against the other, to gain his favour.* Yet was he so different? It was comforting to think that he had the moral courage to face Groshen. Comforting but untrue. *We need him*, he thought. *The weaklings in there, me, others. We need him in order to survive.* And that, after all, was the most important thing. To survive no matter what the cost.

He straightened as the electrostatic barrier opened and Groshen stepped from the steam into the cooler air. He was naked but for a loincloth, muscles bunching, rippling beneath the ebony skin which glistened with a patina of sweat.

He looked at Gyrn. 'News?'

'Nothing fresh, my lord. The members of the Spinners Association have left for their estates. All but Stockholder Hurl.'

'He would naturally stay.' Groshen passed into a room beyond, threw himself on a rubbing couch. 'Well, he won't bother us for long.'

'No, my lord.'

Groshen smiled. 'I like that,' he admitted. 'Soon only I shall be so addressed.' He frowned. 'Or should it be 'master'? No,' he decided. 'That is a term used by slaves. I do not wish to rule a world of slaves.'

'Most men would think that to rule is enough, my lord,' ventured Gyrn.

'Perhaps. But that is the difference between you and me, Commander. You would be happy to rule a pack of dogs. I need to rule a world of heroes.' Groshen stretched as the masseur came to knead his muscles. 'Heroes who acknowledge me their master. Who are waiting to place my foot on their necks.' He stretched again, an animal pleased with its grooming, 'What did you want?'

'There are rumours in the city, my lord. News of the challenge has leaked out. The people demand to know where and when the contest is to be.'

'They will know when I tell them,' said Groshen casually. 'Not before.'

'It would be wise not to delay the announcement, my lord,' said Gyrn evenly. 'There is a natural excitement. I fear for unrest.'

Groshen rolled beneath the hands of the masseur. 'They want to see me beaten,' he said. 'Do you think I don't know their minds? All weak men hate and envy the strong. I am the strongest man on Toy and therefore the most hated. The computation is simple to appreciate.' He looked up as a scarlet shape entered the room. 'In good time, cyber. I need your services.'

'My lord?'

'Gyrn wants me to tell him when and where I shall choose to fight my sister.'

'Not your sister, my lord,' corrected the cyber in his even monotone. 'Her proxy.'

'It is the same. Where I am going to fight Stockholder Hurl and one of his friends.'

Again Creel had to correct the statement. 'It is not they you will be fighting, my lord. The Lady Quara has been clever. She has chosen two others to take her place.'

Groshen sat upright, waved away the masseur. 'Who?' he demanded.

'The two men who fought the weavers at your party, my lord. The same two who escaped death in the arena.'

Groshen smiled without humour. 'So my dear sister is proving herself to be cunning as well as beautiful. What did she offer them, I wonder? Something magnificent to make them walk quietly to their deaths.' His eyes moved to those of the commander. 'Why didn't you know of this?'

Gyrn made a helpless gesture.

'They are keeping it a secret,' said Creel evenly. 'They hope that you will continue to believe you are to be matched against Stockholder Hurl and another, and you will be careless. They are two dangerous men, my lord,' he said. 'Trained to fight and kill.'

'You think I could not beat them?'

'Apart, one at a time, you could beat them,' admitted the cyber. 'But both together at the same time? With respect, my lord, I doubt it.'

Groshen scowled.

'I do not now advise, my lord,' said Creel in his emotionless modulation. 'I predict. In this case my prediction is that, if you face the two of them in normal combat, you will lose. Have I been wrong as yet, my lord?'

Impatiently the Toymaster swung his legs over the edge of the couch. Water blasted over his head and body as he showered away the sweat and oil. Dripping, he glared at Creel as he stood before a drier. 'What do you suggest?'

'The combat cannot be avoided, my lord.'

'I know that,' snapped Groshen. He stepped from before the drier, snatched a robe from the masseur, wrapped himself in purple weave.

'You have the power to choose time, style and place.'

'I know that also.' Groshen blinked, a smile replacing his frown. 'You are clever, cyber. I catch the drift of your thoughts.' His smile widened, turned into a laugh.

'Of course! What better place to fight?'

'My lord?' Gyrn was curious.

Groshen turned to face the commander. 'The Maze, fool! We shall fight in the Maze!'

'And the time, my lord?'

'Three hours from now.'

10

There was a domed entrance, a drop-shaft falling to an artificial cavern half-filled with waiting men. They turned as Dumarest stepped from the shaft, face softened by diffused lighting, eyes gleaming. *Like animals*, thought Dumarest. *Eager and hungry for the kill, the spectacle of men locked in combat.* He frowned as he looked around the cavern. It had a rough, unfinished look as if completed in haste, and he could see no ring, no arena. Where, in this place, would they fight?

Legrain stepped out of the shaft to stand at his side, Quara and Leon following. For a moment they stood at the head of the gentle slope leading to the main area, then Leon led the little party to where a knot of men stood apart from the rest. Vohmis, his face carrying more lines than those caused by age, came to meet them.

'Stockholder Hurl.' Their hands met,

open palm touching open palm, archaic proof that neither intended violence. 'And Stockholder Quara Groshen. It is good to see you, my dear. I could only wish that it was under happier circumstances.' Mournfully he shook his head. 'This is a bad day for Toy.'

She smiled at his concern. 'It could be a good one, Librarian.'

'If the Toymaster is bested? Perhaps? Perhaps. But is it ever good for brother to fight sister?' Vohmis looked at Dumarest and Legrain. 'Are these two men your proxy?'

Quara nodded. 'Help us, Librarian. We received notification only a short while ago. Where and what is this Maze?'

Vohmis glanced to where an opening, ten feet square and filled with milky light, gaped in the wall of the cavern. 'There you see it. Beyond lies a convolution of surfaces impossible to describe. A whim of the Toymaster's,' he explained. 'Built as a plaything. I can tell you no more.'

Legrain made a disgusted sound. 'Is that it?' he demanded. 'Is that where we are to fight?'

'That is correct,' said Vohmis.

Dumarest thinned his lips as he looked at the girl. 'My lady, I do not like this. It puts us at too great a disadvantage. Your brother must know the plan while we do not. Is there no way to change the locale? Force the Toymaster to settle the challenge somewhere else?'

She made a helpless gesture. 'No,' she said. 'He has the right to choose the time and place. We have no choice but to obey. To do otherwise is to lose by default.' She hesitated. 'I did not think he would do this. If you wish — I . . . '

She broke off, turning, tilting her head as a sigh echoed through the waiting crowds. Bright against the background stone, the Toymaster stood on the head of the slope.

He was splendidly barbaric in his wide-shouldered tunic and flared pants all of spotted weave. Brightness sparkled from the metal ornaments on his belt, the butt of his whip, the metal tipping the lash. Others joined him, a cloud of sycophants, the tall scarlet of the cyber. Dumarest stared at the pale shadow of the face beneath the cowl, caught the gleam of watchful eyes. *Like red slime,* he thought. *Grasping, destroying, fouling everything it touches.* He turned away, studying the enigmatic opening as Groshen swept towards them.

'My dear sister,' he purred malevolently. 'How wonderful you look! So charmingly innocent and devoid of guile.' His eyes held dancing mockery. 'How does it feel, dear sister, to send two men to their deaths?'

She met his eyes, his mockery. 'Two, brother? I have never thought of you as twins.'

'You laugh,' he said. 'Well, laugh while you may. In a short while you will have small cause for such humour. You will no longer be a stockholder of Toy. You will be nothing, sister. Nothing!'

She felt Leon's hand on her arm, heard his soft warning. 'Not now, Quara. Do not again lose your temper.'

Do not again make a fool of yourself, she thought bleakly. *That is what he is really saying. Well, he is right. Once should be lesson enough.* Because of it she stood to lose everything she owned. Her eyes rested on Dumarest, on Legrain. *But they will lose even more*, she thought. *They will both shortly be dead.*

Vohmis came bustling forward, intent on procedure, hating what he was doing but determined that it should be done right. 'Gentles,' he called. 'Your attention.' He looked at the contestants. 'You must permit yourselves to be searched for hidden weapons. I apologise for any offence my words may cause and I cast no doubt on your honour, but it is a thing which must be done.' He glanced at the cyber, standing, tall and watchful to one side. 'I ask the cyber to conduct the examination. Does anyone object?'

'No,' snapped the Toymaster.

Vohmis glanced at Dumarest, at Legrain.

'No, said Legrain quickly and then softly, to Dumarest, 'This is getting on my nerves. The sooner we get into action the better.'

Dumarest stood rigid as the cyber searched his body. A gleam of metal shone in one pale hand, the flexible length of the open collar.

Groshen glanced at it and laughed. 'The badge of a slave,' he said contemptuously. 'Let him keep it as a souvenir of happier days.'

'Thank you, my lord,' said Dumarest quietly. 'Now will you please be so good as to remove your whip?'

'This?' The Toymaster lifted his left arm. 'It is a part of my dress.'

'It is still a weapon,' insisted Dumarest. 'And a vicious one.' He bowed as Groshen slipped the loop from his wrist, flung the whip to one of his sycophants.

'Thank you, my lord.'

Groshen scowled, impatiently waited for the examination to be completed. 'I shall not be entering the Maze alone,' he announced. 'The cyber will accompany me. He will take no active part but, as I am to face two men, I insist on a witness.'

Legrain shrugged. 'I've no objection. How about you, Earl?'

'None,' said Dumarest.

'Then it is decided,' said the Toymaster. 'There will be no weapons. We fight bare-handed.' His laughter rolled in echoes from the walls of the cavern. 'And this is what we shall do.' His arm lifted, pointed at the opening. 'You will enter the Maze. In two minutes I shall follow. The time will be checked by the Librarian and these witnesses.' He gestured towards the watching men. 'Somewhere within we shall meet. Whoever survives to emerge will be the victor. Do you understand?'

Dumarest nodded and led the way towards the milky light.

* * *

It was like walking under water, in the centre of a cloud, through a mist of luminous particles. The light came from all sides, dazzling, causing the walls to merge with the roof, the floor with the walls, distorting perspective and destroying orientation. Dumarest stumbled and almost fell as the floor seemed to tilt beneath his feet. He had the odd impression that he no longer walked vertical to the pull of gravity but at an angle impossibly acute.

'This is crazy,' said Legrain at his side. The walls of the tunnel caught the words, threw them back as soft echoes. 'Stupid. Why couldn't we have met in a ring? And no weapons,' he added. 'I don't like that. The Toymaster's an ugly customer to meet on even terms.'

'There are two of us,' reminded Dumarest. 'We'll make out.'

He turned, looked back the way they had come, saw only a swirling haze of light. Continuing, he allowed his companion to take the lead. Ahead the light faded, no longer dazzling but reduced to a wall-trapped glow that destroyed all shadows. Ahead, also, the tunnel split, branching to left and right. Ten yards further each branch split again.

Dumarest paused, frowning. There was no place to hide for a surprise attack. The Toymaster would be able to see at least several yards ahead, from one junction to another, and the light made it impossible to hide.

Legrain called from the left-hand branch. 'Come on, Earl. Let's get moving.'

He headed down the left-hand tunnel. Dumarest followed, dragging his heel hard against the floor. Without hesitation Legrain took the right-hand passage at the next junction. It led sharply downward before splitting. This time he took the left-hand branch, then the right, then the left again.

Dumarest caught his arm. 'Do you know what you're doing?'

Legrain nodded. 'I've been in places like this before,' he said. 'On Hand. They go in for puzzles and labyrinths, run competitions, things like that. Usually there's a rule for finding your way about in a place like this. A formula. Take the first right, second left, second right, first left and back to first right again. It varies, of course, but that's the usual thing.'

'Is that why you're alternating?'

'Not really. But this way we won't get lost. We can always find our way out again.'

Dumarest dropped to his knees and rested his ear against the floor, looking back the way they had come. 'Nothing,' he said, climbing to his feet. 'No vibration at all. They must have chosen the other branch.'

'Or they could be sneaking up on us,' said Legrain. 'I don't know the layout of these passages. The Toymaster does. For all we know he's waiting ahead by now.' He hesitated. 'You know what I think, Earl?'

'Yes,' said Dumarest. 'You're thinking that it would be best if we split up.'

Legrain was defensive. 'It would double our chances of finding him. We could even manage to catch him between us. That's about the only way we're going to get out of this alive,' he said. 'Hit him before he knows it. Attack from front and rear.'

'You could be right,' said Dumarest. 'Can I trust you?'

'All the way,' said Legrain. 'Every step all the time.'

Dumarest smashed his fist against the other's nose. He hit again, feeling cartilage yield, seeing blood spurt over the startled face. His left fist dug into the stomach, right swinging down in a vicious tearing slash to the ear. Legrain staggered back, eyes blazing, hands to his face.

'I owed you that,' said Dumarest coldly.

'For leaving me in that cave.'

'But, Earl! I told you . . . '

'I know what you told me. But I could have been killed climbing up that cliff.' Dumarest reached forward, grabbed Legrain by the shoulder. 'This time, maybe, you won't let me down.' His fingers closed, digging into the flesh. 'Now go and look for the Toymaster. If you find him yell. Keep out of his way and keep shouting until I join you. I'll do the same, Understand?'

Legrain nodded.

'Then move!' Dumarest thrust him away. 'And don't forget what I told you. Let me down again and I'll tear out your throat.'

He walked away, took two right-hand passages, waited, returned, Legrain had vanished. On the floor a pool of blood showed where he had been. Dumarest dropped to his knee and squinted along the floor. He smiled. Against the glow showed dark patches from the blood on the soles of Legrain's boots. Rising, Dumarest began to follow the trail.

It was hard, tedious, the light trapped

in the walls causing his eyes to tire, making the little smears of darkness harder to see. The passages changed, altered in a subtle manner so that they seemed less like the convolutions of a three-dimensional maze than a peculiarly winding path that seemed to defy all normal laws. After a while there was only the one passage, lifting, slipping, twisting and turning apparently in and back on itself.

Dumarest closed his eyes. The passage had somehow merged with others in a visual nightmare of glowing walls and transparent partitions, a jumble of peculiar angles impossible to follow. He felt as if he were falling and yet, at the same time, being crushed beneath a solid mountain of rock. There was a horrible sensation of extension coupled with the certain knowledge that he was being inexorably compressed. The senses of his body were at war with each other, each denying the validity of what the others knew to be true.

He dropped to his hands and knees, crawled along the passage, the floor oddly mobile beneath his weight. It grew solid, reassuringly firm, and he opened his eyes. The nightmare was over. Ahead lay the familiarly glowing walls, the passages of the labyrinth, the telltale flecks of blood.

Dumarest rose, stepped cautiously forward, froze at the sound of echoing voices.

And almost died as hands closed around his throat.

His reaction was instinctive. Muscles corded beneath the hands as he fought the pressure, afraid not of asphyxiation but of the thumbs gouging at his vertebrae. He could live minutes without air but only seconds with a broken neck. Reaching up, he clawed at the little fingers. They resisted as if made of iron. He lifted his right foot and kicked savagely backward. The grip around his throat eased a little as the man moved to avoid the boot. Again Dumarest wrenched at the little fingers, tore them from his neck, pulled savagely backward.

'Clever.' The Toymaster smiled with a flash of teeth as Dumarest spun round. 'Not many men could have broken that grip. Where is your friend?' Dumarest sucked air, not bothering to answer, studying the man he had to kill. Groshen was deceptively casual, a man fully at his ease, confident of his superiority. He laughed, echoes ringing from the walls, the open mouth a red cavern on his face. 'Come, little man,' he urged. 'You are my sister's champion. Must I tell her how easily you died?' He stepped forward, arms extended in a lover's embrace.

Cautiously Dumarest backed away. Groshen was big, powerful, eager and willing to kill. To level the odds it was important to make the first blow tell. To cripple him in some way so as to gain an edge. Dumarest breathed deeply, oxygenating his blood, summoning strength for a major effort. The groin? He doubted it. The target was too small and certainly protected. To try a kick would be to expose his foot and, if he missed, he would be off-balance and at a disadvantage. The knees? Possible, but Groshen wore high boots and the flared pants could contain defensive shielding. The stomach was flat, ridged with muscle, the chest was a reinforced barrel of muscle and bone. He had already felt the strength of hands and arms.

'You are afraid,' said Groshen, moving forward. 'A coward.' He laughed again. 'My sister should see this. How her brave champion retreats at the touch of danger. Do you wish for mercy? Beg hard enough and I may grant it.' His hands lowered, rested on his waist. 'Come now, don't you want to live?'

Dumarest lunged at his throat.

He moved in a blur of motion, stiffened right hand chopping savagely at the side of Groshen's neck, left thumb aimed at the right eye. He felt corded muscle beneath his right hand, softer tissue beneath his left. The Toymaster snarled like a beast as Dumarest struck again at the throat, this time at the larynx. Groshen's hands rose, clenched into fists, pounded like hammers. Dumarest grunted, tasting blood, jerking his knee to the groin as he chopped again at the throat. The knee missed. Groshen stepped back and punched. Dumarest dodged and retreated, fighting for breath.

'Quick,' said the Toymaster. He wiped his face with the back of a hand. Blood ran down his cheek from his injured eye. 'You are fast and cunning but the end is inevitable. You will die in pain.'

He ran forward, arms open to crush Dumarest in their grip. Dumarest caught them, threw himself backward, kicked up with both feet as his shoulders hit the ground. Groshen landed beyond his head. Dumarest rose, kicked again as the Toymaster climbed to all fours, his boot landing beneath the ribs. He might as well have kicked a tree.

Groshen rose, gripped an arm, flung him against the wall. Before Dumarest could recover a fist exploded against his jaw. He sagged, sensed another blow coming and threw himself to one side. Spotted weave showed against the pale glow. He hit out, felt something yield, hit again. A blow sent him staggering, a second made him fall. Desperately he rolled, climbed to his feet, ran down a passage in order to gain time.

He caught a glimpse of a spacious chamber, a tall figure in familiar scarlet,

Legrain's swollen face. Then something smashed against the back of his skull and sent him hard against one wall.

'You!' Groshen, rearing, face smeared with blood from nose and eye, turned to Legrain.

Creel shot the Toymaster dead.

He stood, very calm, looking down at the dead body, the hole charred between the eyes. Slowly he turned and stared at Dumarest, on the floor. 'I told you,' he said to Legrain in his even modulation. 'There had to be a reason for his attack. It was the only way he could follow you. The blood from your injuries left a trail.'

Legrain shifted his feet. 'I don't think so,' he said stubbornly. 'I wouldn't have come here had I thought that.'

'You should have killed him as I ordered,' said the cyber.

'Killed him? How? He didn't give me a chance. He attacked before I was ready.' Legrain stepped forward, looked down at the limp figure. 'He can't do any harm now.'

'No,' agreed the cyber. 'Neither of them can interfere.' He stooped over

Dumarest, lifted an eyelid. 'You are not dead,' he said. 'You are not even unconscious. It is useless to pretend that you are.'

Dumarest opened his eyes. He felt oddly detached, as if he were living in a dream. The watching figures of Legrain and the cyber seemed to swell and diminish. Concussion, he thought. That last blow to the head coupled with the impact against the wall. He sat upright, leaning his back against the glowing surface. He nodded as he saw the Toymaster.

'You had to kill him,' he said. 'You couldn't let him live.'

'The fool had served his purpose,' said Creel. In the shadow of his cowl his face held a glowing satisfaction. He was feeling the only pleasure he could ever experience. He needed to boast of his mental achievements. 'Do you know where we are?' he demanded. 'This chamber is almost touching the machine, the precious Library of Toy. Can you guess why this labyrinth was constructed? For the sole purpose of establishing this nexus. Topography,' he said. 'A unique science. Those passages you traversed covered a great distance in a special relationship with both themselves and the machine. Not one of the local technicians could dream that they were building a device to wreck their economy.'

Dumarest blinked, shook his head, sagged weakly back against the wall. 'The Library,' he said. 'You intend to destroy the Library.'

'That is correct.'

'But how? I mean . . . ' Dumarest broke off. 'Sick,' he muttered. 'Eyes all peculiar. Head hurts and I feel sick.'

'Good,' said Legrain viciously. 'I'd like you to feel more than sick. I'd like to smash your face in, tear out your eyes, let you crawl around in this place until you starve.' He looked at the cyber. 'How about that? I've got it coming for what he did to my nose.'

'No.'

'Too rough for your precious stomach?' Legrain shrugged. 'Well, you're the boss.' His booted foot swung, impacted against Dumarest's side. 'How would you like a few broken ribs?'

'Enough.' Creel had no time for petty revenge. 'It is time for us to prepare.'

Sullenly Legrain began to strip. Naked, he clawed at his stomach, chest and thighs. Surrogate flesh peeled away. The false paunch disguised a cavity that held a coil of heavily coated wire. Gingerly he placed it on the ground.

'A special manufacture of the Cyclan,' said Creel as Legrain dressed. 'There is more energy in that wire than you could imagine. Enough to warp the very structure of space itself. We shall use it to gain access to the machine.'

'They will kill you,' said Dumarest. 'If they ever learn what you intend the stockholders of Toy will tear you apart.'

'True, but they will never learn. Do you think that the plans of the Cyclan are so easily shaken? This has been pondered for years by the finest intelligence in the entire universe. Every step has been planned, every danger predicted, all obstacles overcome.' Creel gestured to the walls of the labyrinth. 'Do you think this was built by chance?'

'The Toymaster built it,' said Dumarest.

He looked at the dead man. 'Built it to die in it, but I'll bet he didn't know that.'

'But who planted the idea in his mind?'

'You,' said Dumarest. 'The Cyclan.'

'True. A traveller, apparently a dealer in amusing constructions, but a person working for an unsuspected end. Unsuspected by Groshen, that is. It was a simple matter to entrance him with the notion of a mysterious Maze. It was logical to have it built by Library technicians and so equally logical to have it built not too far from the machine. The planning of our scientists took care of the rest. Topographically we are very close to the vaults containing the memory banks of the machine. Destroy those and we destroy the independence of Toy.'

Creel took a laser from beneath his robe, a larger model than he had used on Groshen.

Legrain took it. 'Now?'

'At once.'

Legrain walked to the wall of the chamber. It bore markings, a broad cross. Carefully he began to drill into the wall at the marked spot.

Dumarest eased himself against the wall. His fingers touched his pocket, slipped inside, felt the smooth surface of the collar. Legrain turned from where he worked. 'How about letting me use this on Dumarest? I'll feel safer when he's dead.'

'We have no power to waste,' said Creel. 'And what can he do? He has no weapon. I searched him and I know that.' He looked down and addressed the topic of their conversation. 'There you see the workings of an emotion-loaded mind. He yields to petty hates and imagined fears and would risk losing much in order to gain so little. Your death, what can it mean to him? Revenge, what motivation is that? The past is irrevocable. We of the Cyclan do not waste effort in illogical pursuits.'

'You know,' said Dumarest, 'if I were you I wouldn't trust him with that laser. He might kill you just to get me.'

It was wasted effort and he knew it, but he had to try to keep the cyber talking. Again he touched the smooth metal in his pocket. *If it hadn't been for Groshen I'd have had them*, he told himself. *I could have come up and taken them both by surprise. Now the Toymaster's dead and I'm not much better.* Cautiously he tried to move his legs. They obeyed but the effort caused blood to sing in his ears. *My hands*, he thought. *I can use my hands. But will it be enough?*

He looked up, saw the scarlet robe, the cowled face with the watching eyes.

'Will you never understand?' Creel moved his hands a little within the wide sleeves of his robe. 'We of the Cyclan do not leave anything to chance. Our predictions are accurate. That man' — he nodded toward Legrain — 'is our instrument. I know exactly what he will do under any circumstance. He will not harm me. He will not even harm you unless I give permission. That is but a measure of the Cyclan's power.'

'To know,' said Dumarest. 'To always be right.' He gently moved his head. 'But what fun is life if you know what is to come?'

'Almost through,' called Legrain. 'It can't be much further.'

'The machine,' said Dumarest quickly. 'How do you intend to destroy it? By explosives?'

'Nothing so crude. The surrogate flesh that Legrain removed is a mass of electronically treated particles. Once within the vaults we shall release them. They will spread and penetrate into the memory banks. The effect will be total and complete erasure.'

'Through,' said Legrain. 'At least the laser's out of power.' He swung it, pointed it at Dumarest, pressed the trigger. 'See?'

'The wire,' said Creel. 'Quickly.'

Legrain flung down the exhausted weapon and picked up the coil of wire. Gently he began to feed it into the hole he had made. Dumarest watched, frowning. Were they going to operate by remote control?

'The wire is a door,' said Creel. 'Once released the forces it contains will expand the surrounding matter in a line parallel to itself. An adjustment of the atomic arrangement,' he added. 'The practical effect is that the atomic space in the surrounding matter is cleared of obstruction. When the field collapses it will fill the entire area. The substance of the wire, of course, will be used to establish the field.'

He turned, did something to the end of the wire. 'Watch.'

The wire began to glow and then, with shocking abruptness, a hole showed in the wall. It was seven feet in diameter, perfectly round and level with the floor. A gust of cold air came through it, causing Legrain to shiver.

'Come on,' he said. 'Let's not waste time.' He stooped and picked up the surrogate flesh he had discarded and headed towards the opening.

Dumarest slipped his hand out of his pocket. He was holding the collar. His other hand found it, fumbled, joined the ends together. They locked with a soft click.

Creel turned as he stepped into the opening, one hand slipping from his wide sleeve. 'The possibility of your causing any damage is remote,' he said. 'Nevertheless it does exist. Therefore it is logical that I should kill you.'

Dumarest threw the collar.

It glittered as it spun towards the cyber's face. Instinctively Creel stepped back, lifting his hand and firing all in the same movement. He was a good shot. The beam sliced the collar open.

It exploded level with his face.

11

Quara fumed with impatience. 'How much longer?' she demanded, harshly. Her eyes were fastened on the square opening filled with milky light. 'Surely they must have met by now?'

Leon studied her profile. *She's worried,* he thought. *Inside she must be sick with it. And no wonder. Everything depends on who is going to step through that opening.* He felt a sudden wave of protective tenderness. 'Quara,' he said softly. 'Listen to me. No matter what happens you will need for nothing. I promise that.'

She turned and looked into his face. 'You mean if I lose?'

'Yes,' he said. 'If you win there will be nothing you will need from me. Nothing I can give you.'

'Are you so very sure of that?' Her hand found his own, pressed. 'But if I lose, Leon, you will take me beneath your protection? Look after me? Is that what you mean?'

It was a moment for madness. 'I would like to take care of you for the rest of my life.'

'Marry me, you mean?'

The concept was so novel that it shook his self-possession. Never had he thought of her as a wife. As a ward, yes, an adopted child perhaps, but never as a wife. But why not? If the prediction of the machine was correct his lifespan was measured in hours. Marriage would be the best way to protect her. He had no children, so as his widow she would inherit his stock. 'Yes,' he said. 'I am asking you to marry me. It will be a legal technicality, nothing more, but . . . '

She rested the tips of her fingers against his lips. 'Leon,' she said softly, 'Say no more. I'll . . . ' She broke off, startled. 'What was that?'

They had all felt it. A shudder. A dull echo as of a deep-buried explosion. A communicator hummed on the Librarian's wrist. He tripped the switch, listened, stared at Leon with a face suddenly haggard.

'There has been an accident,' he said.

'A detonation in the vaults of the machine.' He looked around, wildly. 'I must get there at once! How . . . '

'There are rafts on the surface.' Leon took charge, sensing that Vohmis was suffering from shock. Damage to his precious machine was a blow to his heart. 'Listen,' he called to the waiting men. 'Remain here. You are witnesses as to the result of the challenge.' He looked at Quara. 'Do you wish to stay here or come with me?'

'With you,' she said quickly, and led the way toward the shaft.

Technicians met them as they landed. In a tight group they entered the Library, a drop-shaft, a car that hummed through a tunnel. The memory banks themselves were miles from the communication panels, deep-buried in solid rock, protected against all possible danger.

Vohmis bit nervously at his nails, 'What happened?' he demanded. 'What caused the explosion?'

'We have no idea, Librarian,' said one of the technicians. 'Our instruments recorded a slight seismological disturbance, some heat and pressure, all at a point in the extreme perimeter of the lower vaults. We have sealed the area.'

'Damage?'

'We are still testing, Fortunately it seems to be confined to the point in question.'

Vohmis nodded, jumped from the car as it came to a halt. 'Hurry,' he ordered. 'I must inspect the damage.'

It could have been worse, thought Leon as he followed Vohmis and his technicians through the sealing barriers. Thick baffle-walls had prevented the shockwave from travelling far beyond the source of the explosion, minimising its effect. But that was bad enough. Vohmis shook his head as he stared at the wreckage. 'Ruined,' he said. 'Utterly ruined.'

Each storage bank was ten feet wide, ten high, a hundred long. Most of the space was taken up with coolant fluids, devices to neutralize fluctuating electronic potential, more to establish a neutral field around the actual data storage system. Now everything was a jumbled mess. The explosion had ripped the protective panelling from its structure, smashed it back into the body of the machine, tore free what it hadn't crumpled. The air was frigid, acrid with chemical taint.

'Ruined,' said Vohmis again. 'Utterly destroyed.'

Leon nodded, passed the shattered mess to the far wall. It was deeply gouged in a conical scoop, the open mouth of a funnel pointing at the storage bank. He leaned forward and touched it. The liberation of tremendous energy had blasted the stone. He frowned, leaned closer. His shadow occluded the apex, revealing a tiny point of light.

He turned to the technicians. 'Bring heavy-duty lasers. Excavation equipment. Hurry! There is something beyond this wall!'

★ ★ ★

The room had changed. The carpet was as thick, the windows as tall and glowing with the same morning light, the odd shapes on the scattered pedestals shining with the same brilliance. Even the ceiling with its depictions of old wars was exactly the same. And yet, Dumarest knew, the room had changed. Once it had been just a place with four walls and luxurious furnishings. Now it contained something new.

Quara smiled at him as he stepped toward where she sat on a couch. Leon was beside her and their hands, as if by accident, were very close. *Love*, thought Dumarest. *They're in love and that's why the room has changed*. He halted before them and inclined his head. 'My lord. My lady.'

'You have things the wrong way around,' said Leon. 'Quara is now mistress of Toy. The majority stockholder — thanks to you,'

'But still a woman,' she reminded. 'And not so long a wife.' Her eyes were luminous as she looked at Dumarest. 'I forced him to keep a promise,' she said. 'One made in a moment of pity. When we broke through that wall and found what we did I read his face. Groshen was dead and you barely alive; I think that he would almost have preferred the opposite.'

'Then you would have needed me,' Leon said.

'I need you now,' said Quara. 'I think I have always needed you. And,' she added, 'if Dumarest and not Groshen had died, how long would we have been man and wife?' Her hand touched his, caressingly. 'Did you think I had forgotten the prediction of the machine? You offered to make me a rich widow, protect me from the anger of the Toymaster and total ruin if he had won, and I loved you for it. But I love you more for wanting me as myself.' She remembered they were not alone. 'My apologies,' she said to Dumarest. 'Come, sit and join us in a glass of wine.'

It was the same that he had had before, ruby shining in the crystal goblet, tart and refreshing to his tongue.

'You are fit?' said Leon. 'You feel no discomfort, no pain?'

'None, my lord.'

'Too much has passed between us for such formality,' laughed Quara. She lifted her glass. 'Come, Earl, a toast. To happiness.'

255

They drank.

'You were very ill,' said Leon to Dumarest. 'You almost died. Stockholder Ledra worked hard to save you.' He smiled at Dumarest's expression. 'She volunteered,' he explained. 'And she is the best physician we have on Toy. She also has the finest equipment available. You had three separate treatments of slow time therapy together with complete medical and surgical attention. You are certain that you feel well?'

Dumarest nodded.

'Then you will not begrudge her the germ plasm she extracted as her fee,' said Leon. 'She insisted, and Stockholder Ledra is a very determined woman.'

'Yes,' said Dumarest. 'I gathered as much.' So she had his seed to twist into peculiar shapes, his characteristics to breed into selected strains. Mentally he shrugged. It was immortality of a kind.

'And now,' said Quara, 'I want to know everything. From the very beginning,' she insisted. 'The whole story.' She sat listening, hand touching that of her husband, both engrossed as Dumarest told what had happened in the Maze. 'The explosion,' she said when he had finished. 'What caused it? And why did we find no trace of the cyber and Legrain?'

'The two are connected,' said Dumarest. He fell silent, remembering the noise, the searing gush of energy, the blasting impact of debris that had brought oblivion. 'Creel had established an opening from the labyrinth to the vaults. Both he and Legrain were in it when I threw the collar. He shot at it, cut it, caused it to explode. The sudden release of energy upset the delicate balance of the field and it collapsed. The displaced matter resumed its original position — but the mass of both men were in the way. They were crushed, literally, to an atomic pulp, but those atoms had to go somewhere. They blasted free in an explosion.' He drank what remained of his wine. 'I was lucky,' he admitted. 'I should have died in the blast. I would have died if you hadn't found me so soon.' He looked at Quara. 'I take it there was no argument as to who had won?'

'None. The Toymaster was dead and he had himself stated the conditions. The one who survived to emerge would be the victor. You were alive and you emerged. The technicians bore witness to where we found you.' Quara lifted the flagon, refilled his glass. 'But I still do not understand why Creel did not kill Groshen earlier. Why leave him, a potential danger, free to wander the labyrinth?'

'Because I also was a potential danger,' explained Dumarest. 'The plan was to leave us both while Legrain and the cyber did what they had intended to do all along. If we met and fought a danger would be eliminated. The survivor, whoever he was, could be eliminated later. But Groshen was lucky. Somehow he stumbled on the route to the nexus. Luck,' he said sombrely. 'Not even the Cyclan has the power to determine the random laws of chance. Creel made a mistake. He wanted the Toymaster dead and should have killed him at once. Legrain made another — he should have killed me.'

'Legrain,' said Leon. 'Why did you suspect him?'

'Because he acted out of character. I could understand him leaving me in the cave — that was the act of a selfish and ruthless man. But he paid money to hire an advocate, staying when he had a chance to leave. That made me suspicious. I pretended to believe his story then and later when he said that the guard had grabbed him to put him inside the cage. But after you had made your bargain with us I tested him. Logically there was no reason why he shouldn't have agreed to run off-world while he had the chance. A man who would desert a companion would have no compunction at breaking a bargain. So there had to be a reason for his staying. I guessed that he was working for someone else and getting highly paid for his services.'

'But he could have died,' protested Quara. 'The Toymaster could have killed him.'

Dumarest shook his head. 'No,' he said. 'He wouldn't have died and he knew it. The man he was working for would see to that.'

Leon was baffled. 'But . . . '

'Who?' demanded Quara.

'The cyber,' said Dumarest. 'Who else?' He gulped his wine, paced the floor. 'The Cyclan,' he said. 'The spreading red slime that fouls everything it touches. Creel was a part of it. Legrain was an agent, nothing more; he would have been paid with death, not riches. I knew,' he insisted. 'When I fought the spiders I knew. I saw Creel sitting behind the Toymaster. It was enough.'

Quara looked at him, eyes soft with her woman's intuition. 'You hate them,' she said. 'They have hurt you terribly in some way.'

'Yes,' he said shortly, not wanting to think about it, to arouse old memories. 'I hate them and I know them. They spread, touching world after world, insinuating their way into a position of power. Oh, they don't rule, not openly, but where you find a cyber you find the power of the Cyclan. And they have power. Subtle, unnoticed, but very real. A word, a prediction, a guiding of opinion. They almost won Toy. Take warning, they will try again and yet again. They do not like the opposition of your machine. It makes you independent, others too.' He paused, looking at his hands. They were clenched, the knuckles white. Slowly he forced them to relax, the fingers to uncurl. 'The Cyclan does not like independence,' he said gently. 'It encourages random behaviour.'

He looked at them, saw the doubt in their eyes, the disbelief. 'You think what happened was because of chance?'

Slowly Leon helped himself to more wine. 'The fightmaster,' he said. 'How did Creel know that he would buy you, set you against the weavers?'

'He knew of the Toymaster's party. Who else but a fightmaster would buy a man of my reputation? How hard would it be to suggest combat sports at the party and how easy would it be to hint that I, a man having escaped from the arena, would provide good sport?'

'And Legrain?' demanded Quara. 'Why was he put in the cage? In a position of danger.'

'No danger,' said Dumarest. 'His bonds were loose and, in a real emergency, he could have pulled free. But that wasn't necessary. Creel knew that I would win. It was a simple prediction, as simple as knowing you would fall into the Toymaster's trap, as knowing that, once you'd done so, you would choose me as your champion.' Again he paced the floor.

'You underestimate them,' he said. 'The power of the Cyclan is frightening even though based on such simple things. The ability to predict a logical sequence of events from a given action. The ability to manoeuvre people like puppets and yet never let anyone suspect they are so controlled. Creel knew exactly what you and I and the Toymaster would do. Legrain was put into the cage so as to be close to me and therefore close to you. The whole series of events were aimed at just one thing: to enable Creel to get to the nexus and destroy the Library.'

'And he knew that the Toymaster would pick him as a companion?' Leon spoke over the rim of his glass. 'That he would be chosen to conduct the examination?'

'The Toymaster needed a guide and

Creel knew the intricacies of the Maze. The search?' Dumarest shrugged.

'Had anyone else been chosen there would have been an objection. Who could be more neutral than a cyber? But you don't believe,' he said. 'You think I speak from personal hate. Perhaps I do; I have no cause to love the Cyclan, but think about it. Think how close they came to destroying your economic stability. To destroying the Library.'

'And, knowing all this, you still entered the Maze and fought for me.' Quara rose, rested her hands on his shoulders, looked into his face. 'You alone saved Toy. How can we ever repay you?'

'We made a bargain,' he said. 'Money and information.' He touched his waist where under refurbished clothing a money belt sagged, heavy with gems. 'I have the money.'

'And now you want the information.' Her hands fell from his shoulders. 'Earl, must you travel? On Toy you could find a home. I will give you enough stock for you to live on equal terms with the richest. Must you leave?'

He was curt. 'Yes, my lady.'

'To continue your search for happiness?' She turned, smiled down at her husband, gently touched his hair. 'For some it isn't so hard to find. We have found it, each within the other; it fills the world. But you?' She looked at Dumarest. 'All this has been an interlude for you,' she said wonderingly. 'An episode of no real importance. A single step on a long journey.'

'We made a bargain, my lady,' reminded Dumarest. 'I have kept my part.'

'And I mine.' Her white teeth bit at her lower lip. 'Earl, my friend, I am sorry but . . . '

'You have no information?'

'A little but not enough. Vohmis himself gave the order for the search. That was before you entered the Maze. There is a tight schedule, others had priority, there seemed to be no urgency.' She took a deep breath. 'They were asking about your planet when the explosion occurred.'

He felt a tightness at his stomach. 'And?'

'The memory bank containing the

information was destroyed.'

He had known it; somehow he had guessed. The tightness vanished to be replaced by a hard knot of despair. So close! So very close!

'Something was gained,' Quara said gently. 'Very little, I'm afraid. Only a name.'

'Another name for Earth?'

'Yes. Terra. You have heard of it?'

Dumarest shook his head.

'Perhaps it derives from 'territory',' she suggested. 'Or is a distortion of the word 'terrible' or 'terror'.' She hesitated, 'You did say that it was a bleak world scarred by ancient wars.'

'Very scarred,' he said heavily. 'By wars very ancient.'

'Earl, I'm sorry!' Her sympathy was genuine. 'I've let you down so badly while you . . . ' She blinked eyes suddenly a little too bright. 'The technician gained the second name and was running a check in order to determine the spatial coordinates. He found no correlation in the system in present use. The explosion came before he could extend his investigations and since then the reply has been negative owing to insufficient data. Cross-checks have determined that the information, if available at all, would have been stored in the destroyed memory bank.'

'Thank you, my lady,' said Dumarest. 'At least you tried.'

'Tried and failed,' she said. 'If only I'd tried earlier. Insisted on full priority. Such a little thing,' she added. 'A few hours. Minutes even.'

'Please do not distress yourself, my lady.' Dumarest forced a smile. 'After all, there is no proof that the information was available at all. The memory bank might have contained nothing of value.'

'You are being kind, Earl. Kinder than I deserve.'

No, he thought, not that. She meant well in her fashion and it was true, there had been no apparent urgency. No one could have foretold the explosion. Certainly no one, not even the cyber, could have known the importance of that particular storage bank. But not all had been lost. He had a second name to help his search and he had money with which to travel. What use to regret what might have been?

Leon, watching, had quietly poured wine, emptying the flagon. He handed a glass to the girl, another to Dumarest. Holding a third, he rested his arm about her shoulders. 'Earl, you make me feel oddly guilty,' he said. 'A man rarely achieves such happiness as I have gained. I have Quara and, in her, I have everything. But you? What have you?'

Dumarest looked at his wine.

'He has his quest,' said Quara gently, understanding. 'His reason for living. Above all he still has that.' She raised her glass. 'And, one day perhaps, he too will find his happiness, Let us drink to that.'

Dumarest swallowed the bittersweet wine.

THE END

We do hope that you have enjoyed reading this large print book.

Did you know that all of our titles are available for purchase?

We publish a wide range of high quality large print books including:
Romances, Mysteries, Classics
General Fiction
Non Fiction and Westerns

Special interest titles available in large print are:
The Little Oxford Dictionary
Music Book, Song Book
Hymn Book, Service Book

Also available from us courtesy of Oxford University Press:
Young Readers' Dictionary
(large print edition)
Young Readers' Thesaurus
(large print edition)

For further information or a free brochure, please contact us at:
Ulverscroft Large Print Books Ltd.,
The Green, Bradgate Road, Anstey,
Leicester, LE7 7FU, England.
Tel: (00 44) **0116 236 4325**
Fax: (00 44) **0116 234 0205**

Other titles in the
Linford Mystery Library:

PROJECT JOVE

John Glasby

Norbert Donner and Project Director Stanton work on Project Jove, observing the robots in the Jupiter surface lab by means of the Fly, a remote-controlled exploratory ship. Then Senator Clinton Durant arrives from earth convinced Stanton is hiding something on Jupiter's surface. And, unconvinced of dire warnings of danger, he and his assistants ride a Fly down to question the surface lab robots. They soon find themselves completely at the mercy of the giant planet and its devastating storms . . .

THE STELLAR LEGION

E. C. Tubb

Wilson, a waif of the war of unity, spends his boyhood in forced labour. When he is sent to the penal world of Stellar, he survives, winning promotion in the Stellar Legion, a brutal military system. Laurance, Director of the Federation of Man, wants to dissolve the Legion. He pits his wits against its commander, Hogarth. He's terrified lest the human wolves, trained and hardened in blood and terror, should ravage the defenceless galaxy . . .

ENDLESS

John Russell Fearn

It's June 30th. And in Annex 10, situated in the Adirondack Mountains of New York, scientist Dr. Gray and his team can hardly believe their instrument readings. It's four o'clock, and as the seconds pass, they see that chaos looms for mankind. The Earth is growing hotter, temperatures rocket, as the sun shines through the night and causes endless days. Everyone suffers — the rich, the poor, the criminal and the family man. Will it ever end?

EIGHT WEIRD TALES

Rafe McGregor

A curious woman investigates the dark secrets harboured within the ancient chapel of a ruined signal station. An antique ivory hunting horn will spell the downfall of Professor Goodspeed. Meanwhile, an eldritch voice draws a lonely man ever closer to the drowned town of Lod . . . Eight short tales, each directly inspired by a master of the mysterious or supernatural — Arthur Conan Doyle, H.P. Lovecraft, Anthony Hope, or M.R. James — which will send chills down your spine . . .

STARDEATH

E. C. Tubb

Ships disappear within hyperspace, victims of faster than light travel. But when a lost ship is found, the wreckage reveals that a terrible event has occurred. The lucky ones on the lost ship are dead. The others, turned inside out in a gruesome parody of human beings, are still alive. Captain Kurt Varl commands the mission to discover the cause of this disaster — but the enemy is unknown and Varl must use himself as bait to discover what happened.

SEND FOR DR. MORELLE

Ernest Dudley

Mrs. Lorrimer telephones Doctor Morelle claiming that she's in imminent mortal danger. In the morning her orange drink was poisoned, then she'd found a deadly snake in her bed and now toxic gas is emanating from the chimney and into the room! But is she really in danger? Is she mad — or perhaps feigning madness? Dutifully, Doctor Morelle sets off to the woman's house with Miss Frayle, his long-suffering assistant, who will soon begin to wish she'd stayed behind . . .